MAYBE THIS TIME

by

Chantal Fernando

CHANTAL FERNANDO

Published October 2013
Cover design © Arijana Karčić, Cover It! Designs
Edited by Arijana Karčić

MAYBE THIS TIME is a work of fiction. All names, characters, places and events portrayed in this book either are from the author's imagination or are used fictitiously. Any similarity to real persons, living or dead, establishments, events, or location is purely coincidental and not intended by the author. Please do not take offence to the content, as it is FICTION.

Trademarks: This book identifies product names and services known to be trademarks, registered trademarks, or service marks of their respective holders, The authors acknowledges the trademarked status in this work of fiction. The publication and use of these trademarks is not authorized, associated with, or sponsored by the trademark owners.

ACKNOWLEDGEMENTS

Thank you to my family!

My **husband** and **kids** who support my dream, my sister **Tenielle** who I wouldn't be able to function without. My baby sister **Sasha**. My sister in law **Stacey**, who has always been there for me and is one of the strongest women I have ever met. My parents.

I love you all!

Thank you as usual to **Ari** at **Cover it Designs**. I could gush about this girl all day long- she is that amazing. I've never met anyone who is so willing to go out of their way to help others before. I don't think I know anyone who works harder either. Love you Ari!

Yes, I'm a huge fan girl.

Kara Brown - I would be lost without you. Seriously. You put so much effort into helping me and I'm so grateful.

Jay Mclean - Love our daily chats! Thanks for always being there to listen to me rant, or answer my many questions about completely random topics. You're also pretty damn hilarious ;)

Ahkash - Thank you for doing my site for me. You're still my pole.

Haajira - Thank you boobie for reading all my books☺ Sixteen years and counting!

A huge thank you to all the **blogs** that support and promote me! Here are just a few:

Tsk Tsk What to Read, Promiscuous Book Blog, Three Chicks and Their Books, Jenee's book blog, Nerd Girl, Mommy's Late Night Book-up, Sassy Mum Book Blog, Forever Me Romance, One More Chapter, Natasha is a Book Junkie, B's Beauty and Books Blog, Best Books, Smexy Bookaholics, Book Addict Mumma, Jacqueline's Reads, Love Between the Sheets.

To my beta readers.

Kara Brown, Stephanie Knowles, Alice Priday, Antoinette Smith, Aileen Day and Tawnya Peltonen.

I'm thankful for each of you.

DEDICATION

To my three little alpha males in training.

"My heart lies vulnerable outside my chest."
– Kresley Cole

MAYBE THIS TIME

CHAPTER ONE

Summer

This isn't exactly how I expected to meet him for the first time.

I wait outside the jail, nervously glancing around as if someone could mug me at any second.

And they probably could.

Finally, after an hour of waiting, he walks out. He's tall and muscular, with a familiar head of light brown hair. His stride is confident, sure. A smile quirks his full lips when he sees me, and he instantly quickens his pace. As he steps right in front of me, I stare into hazel eyes that are so different from my own dark brown.

"Summer," he says, his eyes crinkling with warmth. I huff out a sigh, trying to look put out, but then fall into his embrace the second he opens his arms to me. I squeeze him tight, not wanting to let go.

He smells like cigarettes and leather, but I couldn't care less.

"'Bout time you came home," he says, rubbing my back.

"I know, I just felt guilty," I say truthfully, pulling from his embrace. If my mother was alive, she wouldn't want me to be here.

"You have no reason to feel guilty. Come on, let's get out of here."

I nod and watch as my brother gets into my car.

*****

"You going to tell me why I had to pick you up from jail?" I can't stop myself from asking.

"Misunderstanding," is all he tells me. It's a bit late for me to play the big sister role, so I don't ask him anything else. Instead I sigh, and ask him for directions to his house.

Xander is only a year younger than me, but this is the first time I've met him in person. I can't help glancing at him from the corner of my eye every now and again, taking in his every movement, his every feature. His hair is long, almost to his shoulders, and he has a dimple in his chin. He's covered in tattoos, with two full sleeves and even a few peeking out from under his collar. His knuckles are split open, like he'd gotten into a fight recently.

I've waited for this day for years, but now that it's here I'm not quite sure what to say or do.

"You might wanna keep your eyes on the road," he says, amusement lacing his tone. I don't answer him, but turn my head forward. Xander leans forward and puts the CD player on. Drake's 'Started from the Bottom' starts to play, and I can feel his amused gaze on me. He skips to the next song, which happens to be 'How Do You Want It' by 2pac. He turns the music off and the rest of the drive is quiet.

2

"Turn left here, and keep going." I follow his instructions, glad for the distraction.

"Right here, Summer. It's the third house on the left," he says, pointing.

"Okay. Dad won't be here, will he?" I ask quietly after we pull up in the driveway to a large brick house.

Not what I was expecting at all.

Xander flashes me an unreadable look. "No, he's not here." I exhale in relief. No way am I ready to see him just yet.

"Open the boot and I'll get your bags," Xander offers. My brother is chivalrous, interesting. Looks like my mother was wrong about him in so many ways.

I lean against the car, playing with the rips in my distressed jeans as he takes out my bags. He starts to walk towards the house, dragging my pink leopard print suit case with him. I bite my lip, trying not to laugh at a rough looking man covered in tattoos with such a girly accessory. Xander turns around when he realizes I'm not following him, and raises an eyebrow in question.

I reluctantly take a step towards the house.

Towards my new life.

My temporary new life, or so I've been telling myself. Xander opens the door wide for me to enter, and I hesitantly step in behind him.

This is the house that Xander grew up in, with my father.

Our father.

And I'd never even seen it until today. My greedy eyes take every detail in, until my gaze stops on Xander watching me closely.

"Your room is the first on the right." I don't know what he saw when he looked at me, but it caused him to soften.

"Okay," I say, heading towards my room.

"I'll go out and get us some dinner. Make yourself at home, Summer," I hear him say behind me.

I nod, even though he can't see it.

The house might be older, but inside it looks modern and welcoming. My room is spacious, especially compared to my old room. My mother may have been financially stable but there was just the two of us, so we shared a three bedroom apartment. It was in a good area, but the rooms weren't large like the one I'm standing in right now. The bed is a queen size, surrounded by a wooden heard board and side tables. There's a dressing table with a huge mirror, and two sets of drawers. Opening the wardrobe, I find more drawers, and space to hang my clothes. A lot of space. There's an unopened set of pink sheets for the bed in the cupboard, along with new pillows and a doona. I grin, imagining Xander shopping for these items for me.

After a long shower, I dry myself and tie my brown hair up in a messy bun. Wrapping the towel around myself, I walk from the bathroom to my room.

I'm almost at my bedroom door when I scream.

I pull the towel higher, and take a few steps back, looking around for a weapon.

4

Anything.

"Fuck, I'm sorry. I'm not going to hurt you," comes an amused drawl. He puts his hands up in a calming gesture.

"Who are you?" I demand, narrowing my eyes.

"Dash!" I hear Xander call out as he walks around the corner. He pauses when he sees us, and shoots a glare at Dash.

"What the fuck are you doing staring at my sister like that?" Xander practically growls. I look at Dash, who is indeed eye-fucking me, and not being subtle about it one bit. Dash throws a crooked smile my way, before turning his violet coloured eyes at my brother.

"You didn't tell me how fucking hot your sis was," he says in a deep rumble. I roll my eyes and walk around him and into my room, slamming the door behind me. I hear his masculine chuckle, along with Xander hissing something about Dash keeping his dick in his pants.

I dress in worn jeans and a black tank top, and head out into the kitchen. I see Xander and Dash in what looks like a heated conversation, all hushed whispers and hand gestures. Feeling a little awkward, I almost want to head back into my room.

"Come and eat, Sum," Xander says when he sees me. He pushes a pizza box towards me, and I also notice some beers on the table. Dash's gaze is on me as I open the pizza box and take out a giant slice of pepperoni. My favourite.

"Does Jack know she's here?" Dash asks Xander, his eyes still glued to me. Xander runs his hand though his hair, looking a little worried.

When Xander rang me, asking me to move in here with him, I told him that I was reluctant because of my father. He doesn't know me, at all, and it feels awkward that he would suddenly want to be in my life after all these years with only making an appearance once a year at most. The truth was, I wanted to be with Xander. I'd wanted to get to know him my whole life, and when he rang me, telling me that if I didn't get here he was going to drive up there to get me himself, I decided it was time. Time to break free.

There was no point staying at home anymore, in my small rental apartment where mum and I used to live. So I quit my waitressing job and left everything and everyone I'd known my whole life behind. All for my brother.

"Yeah, he knows," he answers, his tone and look telling Dash to shut up. I look at Dash. I'm not going to lie, he's ruggedly handsome. Dark hair, piercing violet eyes and a perfectly sexy amount of stubble on his face. I see a matching pair of dimples pop up when he flashes me a flirty smile. I roll my eyes at him, feigning non-interest. The twinkle in his eyes calls my bluff.

"How long are you here for?" Dash asks me, picking up his own slice of pizza.

"Forever," Xander says, the same time I answer, "not long."

My brother pins me with a harsh glare. "What do you mean not long? This is your house, too!"

"No, it isn't, Xander," I say softly. This is his house, and his alone. I know my father gave it to him. I want to spend some time with my brother, and get on my feet, then I can find my own place to live.

"Summer, you have to know that-"

"It doesn't matter. I don't want to be in your way," I tell him, cutting him off.

"Is it cos all of that shit your mother said about me? You don't think that you're safe here?" he asks me, his voice mocking, but his eyes shine with hurt. My whole life my mother has been telling me my brother is a low life. A thug, a criminal, a waste of space. I've heard it all. She tried her best to turn me against Xander and my father, tried to instil it into me from the beginning. I had no idea that he knew about the things she told me. I don't think he cares what she thinks, but from the look in his hazel eyes I can see that he does care about what I think.

"If I listened to everything my mother said I wouldn't be here right now, Xander," I tell him truthfully. He shakes his head, staring down at his feet in annoyance. Dash is watching him, a thoughtful look on his face.

"She told me you were a biker. Is it true?" I blurt out. The two of them eye each other, almost like they are having a silent conversation. I shrug, grab a beer and head to the couch, turning on the TV.

"How old are you, baby?" Dash asks me. Baby?

I take a slow sip of my beer before I reply. "What's it to you?"

"Xander is eighteen, so you must be, what, nineteen?"

"And how old are you?" I ask.

"Older," is all he says. I give him a once over. I'd say he's about twenty five.

"You must be, what, thirty?" I ask, pursing my lips so I don't laugh when I see his reaction.

He narrows his eyes. "I don't look that old."

"Of course not," I say, dragging the words out.

He opens his mouth to say something else, when two men walk into the house.

Does no one even knock? Or believe in locking doors?

I peer up at them, surprised to see that they are twins. Identical twins. Both have blonde hair, and bright blue eyes. The only difference I can spot between them is the scar one of them has, marring the right side of his cheek. It looks like it might have been made by a knife, and runs deep along his jaw line. His hair is shaved on both sides, and a little longer on the top, while the other has his hair longer and messier, falling charmingly over his forehead.

"Anyone ever tell you it's rude to stare?" the scarred twin says with a growl.

"Reid," the other twin says, a warning in his tone.

"Summer, this is Reid and Ryan," Xander introduces as he sits down on the couch opposite me.

"This is your sister? Holy fuck," Ryan says with a smile. Reid just glares at me, brooding. He seems... charming.

"Yeah, and she's off limits," Xander says, his eyes on the TV.

"Where's the fun in that?" Ryan says, sitting down next to me. He nudges me playfully with his elbow, and I can't help it when my lips curve into a smile. I turn to look at Dash, currently staring daggers at Ryan, his fists clenched. Having no clue what his deal is, I turn back to Ryan.

"Nice to meet you, Ryan," I tell him. And I mean it. Ryan may seem flirty but I can tell he's harmless. Reid, on the other hand - let's just say I wouldn't wanna meet him in a dark alley any time soon.

"Jack said we all gotta be at the warehouse in an hour," Reid says, still standing, his arms crossed against his muscular chest.

"Warehouse?" I repeat, looking at Xander for answers. I eye all four men warily.

And they all ignore me.

"Alright, we'll be there, don't worry," Xander says, looking at Reid.

"He wants us *all* there," Reid says, looking straight at me.

"I'm not going anywhere." I cross my arms over my chest in protest.

"Just fucking great," Reid mutters, his eyes darting to Xander.

"What?" I ask.

"Of course you'd be an uptight princess," he says, looking pissed off.

I blink once. "Fuck you." I draw out each word.

"No, thanks," he replies, standing there with his feet shoulder width apart, his arms crossed.

My eyes widen at his response. "I'll take you up on that offer," Ryan says, scowling at Reid before flashing me a charming smile. A charming smile that I can imagine has worked on many before me.

"Can you guys not chase her away, please?" Xander says, rubbing his hand down his face.

Something works behind Reid's eyes. "Let's get ready to head out."

Taking that as my cue to leave, I stand up and head to my room. I close the door quietly, although I want nothing more than to slam it with all my might. I lie down on my bed, pulling out my e-reader.

Time to tune out the world.

Reid

Jack's daughter is hot.

No, she's beautiful. Of course she's fucking beautiful.

Jack's told us we need to treat her like she's family. Protect her.

And sure as hell not fuck her.

I think my dick needs to get the memo, because as soon as I saw her, it was standing to attention.

Full attention.

Big brown eyes and pouty lips begging to be kissed. She is a stunner. And her body - holy shit.

She has a body made for sin, huge tits, a tiny waist and hips that flare out. Her ass is round and heart shaped, with a lot to grab onto.

"Stop being a dick to her," Xander warns, causing my lip to twitch.

10

"Jack wants to see her," I tell Xander. I glance towards what I assume is the door to her room. I see Ryan eyeing me curiously, and I hate that he knows me so well. I don't normally give a fuck what others think of me, of my scar. But when Summer was looking at me, I couldn't help but lose my temper. When there are two exact versions of a person, and one is scarred, who do you think the women go for? Don't get me wrong, I get my fair share of those who want to take a ride on the wild side. Summer doesn't seem like that type, though. I don't think she's anything like the women I'm used to.

I don't know how to feel about that.

"I'm not going to force her to go, she just got here," Xander narrows his eyes at me. He loves his sister, that much is clear. I know they've never met before, but Jack told me Xander had managed to write and call her over the years. Her mum was some vindictive bitch that wouldn't let them near her, ever since Jack cheated on her. Not only did Jack cheat but the woman, Daria, got pregnant with Xander. Summer's mother was pissed and took Summer away for good. There's probably more to the story, but that's all that I know.

"Tell Jack I'll bring her when she's ready, he'll understand," Xander says.

"Fine, you explain," My eyes dart to her door once again.

"Someone's going to need to stay here with her, I don't wanna leave her alone," Xander says.

"Reid can stay, he's already seen Jack," Ryan offers, a smile playing on his lips. Xander looks at me warily, but then gives a slight nod.

"Fine, let's go. I'll go and say bye to her," Xander says, standing up and walking over to her room.

"How long have we got?" Dash asks the room.

"Two weeks," I reply. Dash nods and stands up, heading out the front door.

"Two weeks, huh," Ryan says.

"Yeah, I don't know how Jack is going to keep Summer away from this shit," I say, looking down at my feet.

"We'll make it work," my brother says, forever the optimist.

"We're going to have to."

Summer

I walk out of my room after unpacking everything in my suitcase. I freeze when I see Reid sitting on the beat up leather couch, slowly sipping on a beer.

"Why are you here?" I ask bluntly, walking to the fridge to get a bottle of water.

"Xander wanted someone to stay and keep you company," he replies, eyes still on the TV.

"So he chose you?" I scoff.

"You got a problem with that?" he grates out, sounding irritated.

"No, sir," I say sarcastically, closing the fridge with a push of my hip. Reid instantly turns his head, staring at me blatantly.

"What?" I ask, walking over to the couch and taking a seat opposite him. Reid rubs his temple, like I'm giving him a migraine, and doesn't answer. My gaze roams lower, down to his muscular arms. He looks so strong, so masculine. I almost sigh in appreciation when I see how his T-shirt dips into a v, showing off a hint of his toned chest. Yum.

"Yes, we all know I have a fucked up face, you don't need to stare," he snaps, averting his eyes to the TV. A muscle ticks in his jaw, his posture stiff.

"Actually, I was thinking how sexy you are," I say honestly, giving him another once over. He turns to look at me, surprise evident on his face. His eyes widen, and then narrow, as if he finally gets what I said.

"But even your sexiness doesn't cover for your personality, or lack thereof," I say in a saccharine sweet tone.

He studies me for a second. "You're going to be trouble, I can tell," he mutters under his breath.

"Me? I keep to myself, how can I be trouble?" I ask, scowling.

His lip quirks into a crooked smile. "We'll see."

"Cryptic much?" I say, narrowing my eyes a little.

He changes the subject. "Your brother and father love you, a lot. Don't hurt them, Summer."

I gape. "You're kidding me, right?"

He gives me a look that says he's anything but kidding. "If you leave all of a sudden, they're going to be heartbroken. They've been talking about you ever since I've known them."

"Right, so they are the victims in all of this." My voice sounds bitter even to my own ears.

His eyes soften. "No one's gotta be a victim. I'm just saying, they are good men, and you are their weakness."

"I highly doubt that," I say. "I've wanted to meet Xander my whole life. He's the reason I'm here."

"And Jack?" he asks, studying me.

"You're nosy, you know that?"

He shrugs, and tilts his head to the side. "I protect those I care about."

"No one needs protecting from me," I say defensively.

"Maybe so," he says, turning his head. "They seem to think you're the sweetest thing, but I know there's some fire in you."

"You're making assumptions based on what, the whole thirty seconds you've known me?"

His expression doesn't change, but he stands up. "Do you want something to drink?"

I blink once. "Umm, sure." I watch as he goes into the kitchen, and opens the fridge.

"What would you like?"

"Apple juice, please." He pours me some juice and brings it over to me, handing me the glass. Our fingers touch as I take it, and my body instantly reacts, my fingers tingling. As soon as I grasp the glass he pulls his hand away, frowning slightly.

"Thanks," I say, sipping the drink.

He looks at me once more, his blue eyes not missing a thing. I suck in a breath, feeling those eyes penetrate my defences. He opens his mouth to say something, but stops himself. Instead, he gives me a half shrug and returns his gaze to the TV. When he doesn't attempt any more conversation, I mumble a goodnight and head to my room.

CHAPTER TWO

I wake up the next morning and stare at the ceiling. I spent the night tossing and turning, unable to rest. I pick up my phone from the side table and send a quick message to my best friend back home, Lilly. I hear someone moving around in the kitchen, so I drag myself out of bed, desperate for some caffeine.

"Morning," I mumble to Xander, who is standing shirtless in the kitchen, drinking some orange juice straight out of the carton.

"Morning, sis. Coffee?" he asks, offering me a grin.

I nod eagerly. "Yes, please."

I watch as he makes me a coffee, asking how I like it. "Black, please," I tell him.

"Same as me," he says, smiling. He slides it towards me.

"Thanks." I grab the cup and hold it between my hands. "You work out a lot?" I ask him, as I blow on the coffee.

Xander flexes his biceps, and I laugh. He's pretty ripped.

"Yeah we have a small gym set up that we all use." He puts the carton back into the fridge.

I wrinkle my nose at him. "Where do you work?" I ask, realizing I really don't know much about him.

Xander suddenly looks uncomfortable. "Jack has a business or two, I work for him."

"I see." But I really don't. What sort of businesses would my father own?

"What do you wanna do today?" Xander asks me, his eyes sliding to mine.

"I need to find a job."

"You don't need to find work straight away, Summer, I can take care of you," he says in a gentle tone.

"I'm pretty sure that's meant to be my line," I say, my lips twitching.

"Why, cos you're a year older?" he says, amusement lacing his tone.

"Yes."

"I'm the man, sweetheart. You're my sister, I'll take care of you," he tells me earnestly, his eyes now serious.

"I need to find a job, Xander, what else am I going to do around here all day?"

"You could study something, find something you like," he offers.

"I do wanna study something, but I'm going to work, too," I tell him, taking a seat on the bar stool.

"You're stubborn," he says with a sigh. "Another thing we have in common."

"Really? And here I was thinking the only thing we had in common was our extremely good looks," I wiggle my eyebrows at him.

He tilts his head back, laughing. "That too, Summer, that too."

"What's so funny?" Reid asks as he walks into the house. I instantly stiffen, aware I'm wearing only short shorts and a cami.

Great, just great.

"Does no one knock when they come to this house?" I ask. No one answers.

"Go get dressed, Summer," Xander says quietly, his tone demanding. I roll my eyes, but walk to my room, grabbing my clothes to change into. I head for the bathroom, taking a quick shower and brushing my teeth.

I dress in a figure hugging pair of jeans and a peach knit sweater, giving my hair a quick iron so it stays in place. My hair is neither straight nor curly, so I choose to go with one or the other.

When I walk out, conversation ceases. I see Dash is now here as well, leaning against the wall, knee up.

"Where's Ryan?" I ask, since he seems to be the only one missing. I see Reid scowl, his eyes flashing.

"Don't worry your little head, he'll be here," he snaps, his expression shuttered.

Okaaaaaay, then.

"Charming," I mutter to myself as I walk towards my brother.

"Morning, Summer," Dash says, his eyes roaming all over my face and body.

"Hey, Dash." I offer him a small smile. He looks hot wearing a pair of dark jeans and a black T-shirt.

"I'm going to do some grocery shopping," I tell them, searching through my handbag for my car keys. The pantries are practically bare and the fridge only has leftover pizza, beer and some limes.

Which I assume are for tequila shots.

"Wait, I'll come with you," Xander says.

"I think I can handle going to the store without a babysitter," I tell him, giving him my best 'I dare you to say otherwise' look.

"Yeah, but do you know where it is?" He smirks, leaning back against the fridge.

"Surely it can't be that hard to find," I say, rolling my eyes. I finally find my keys and pull them out.

"I can take you," Dash offers. My eyes find Reid, who looks delicious himself in a snug pair of worn jeans and a black sweater. I swallow hard. His body is just phenomenal. Broad shouldered and lean hipped, the man has the perfect amount of muscle. When I glance up into amused blue eyes, I cringe. The last thing I want is for him to think I'm interested in any way.

I clear my throat and tear my gaze away from him. "I'll be fine, but thanks, Dash," I say, waving to them before walking out of the house.

I glance around the neighbourhood quickly, before getting into my car. Pulling out my phone, I look for the nearest supermarket, which turns out to be only about five minutes away. I frown when I see the neighbour peeping over the fence, blatantly staring. He quickly ducks when he sees me looking. I shake

19

my head and drive off, deciding to detour and get familiar with the area.

Reid

"You sure it's safe for her to go out alone?" I ask Xander, not so sure about it myself.

"She'll be fine, it's just down the road and no one knows who she is."

"Yet," I say, knowing it's what everyone else in the room is thinking.

"No one will mess with her," Dash says confidently. Too confidently, and that's his weakness. I try to keep one step ahead, while Dash relies on his reputation way too much. It's true, I'm probably being paranoid. But we do have enemies, and it's always better to be safe than sorry.

"That a gamble you willing to take?" I ask the room. Xander curses, and instantly goes into his room, coming out minutes later fully dressed.

"I can go keep an eye," I offer. The minute the words come out of my mouth I regret them. It's not my job to babysit her. Nor should I want to. Fuck.

"I got it, she's my sis, my responsibility," he says, but he's wrong. She's all of ours, because Jack made her be. Xander leaves in a hurry, now worried about Summer. I'm sure she's fine, there's just a few things she doesn't know about this town.

About her father.

About us.

I think someone needs to update her, and quick. But hell, what do I know? This is their decision to keep her in the dark, and it's not really my business. I suppose if she was mine, I'd want to keep her safe and away from all of this, too.

Then why do I feel slightly guilty?

"Where's Ry?" Dash asks, looking up from his phone, pulling me from my thoughts.

"At the gym, I'm heading there now before work." Ryan and I own our own bar, Knox Tavern. It's just a small pub, but it's ours and we do okay for ourselves. I'd like to think my mother would be proud of us if she were around.

"Alright. I'm going to stick around and wait for Summer." He's trying to appear casual, but I see the way his eyes flicker to mine before he looks back down at his phone.

"You know she's off limits, right?" I can't stop myself from asking.

"Do you?" he replies.

"Not my type," I answer without hesitation. Dash mulls my comment over, before nodding in agreement.

"You're right about that. Summer's a good girl," he says, a wistful smile on his face. It pisses me off. Fuck! She's only been here one night and she's fucking with my head already. With my control.

So what if she's hot? I've had a lot of hot. Sweet, not so much, but only because I generally go for women who know what they're getting into with me. They have no misconceptions of love, romance or forever. They use me, and I use them. We both have a good time, no harm, no foul.

Summer seems like the romance kind. The kind of woman who would try to change a man like me.

I'm not changing for a pretty face.

No matter how stunningly beautiful that face is.

Summer Kane isn't for me.

Summer

"What's up with your neighbour?" I ask curiously, as we carry the last set of bags from the car. I might have gone a little overboard with the groceries, but I figure I'll end up cooking for all the guys anyway. They seem to be a permanent fixture in the house.

"What do you mean?" Xander asks. I found him in the car park of the supermarket I was at, and he said he wanted to make sure I found it okay. My brother is turning out to be a really sweet guy. How wrong my mother was.

"I dunno. Nothing," I tell him, looking over the fence. Xander shrugs. The only person still in the house is Dash, who is texting on his phone, a movie running in the background.

"I'm going to head to the gym. You going to see Jack today?" Xander asks, his tone nonchalant, but his eyes plead with mine.

"What's the big deal?" I ask, wondering why everyone's being so pushy.

"Come on, he hasn't seen you in two years. He wants to see you, Summer."

"And a few more days won't kill him," I say, before leaving the living area.

My father is a tough subject for me to discuss. I don't know him at all. Sure I'd seen him over the years, once a year to be accurate. My mother let him visit every year on my birthday and then I wouldn't see him again until the next. Even when he did visit, the look on my mother's face made me wish he'd just leave. She'd get angry and moody, but mainly bitter. My mother hated my father, but she loved him, too. I know that, because so much hate had to stem from somewhere. When he cheated on her, he turned her love to hate.

Her adoration to scorn.

My mother loved me, but she also loved to remind me daily what a piece of shit my father was for what he did to her, and what a menace Xander was. I don't know where my mother got her information from, but she always had news for me about my brother and all the trouble he was getting into. It used to hurt, a lot. I don't think my mother knew how it affected me, because she was consumed by her hate. But it hurt me every day to have her say cruel things about my own flesh and blood, about the brother I hadn't even met but already loved. She let her bitterness take over and control her, and then she passed away without loving another man.

Jack Kane was it for her.

Apparently he was *it* for a lot of other women, too. I sigh heavily and lie down on my bed on my stomach. I need to find a job, and stat. I have a bit of money saved away, plus what's left of my mother's insurance money, but I can't rely on that for long. I was saving it for a rainy day. My father had also opened a bank account for me, with all the child support he paid over the years, but I hadn't touched that. Not one cent.

To be honest I don't really know how to feel about it. My mother came from a wealthy family and money was never an issue growing up. She used to tell me that the best thing a man can do for his children is love their mother, and he didn't do that for me. He didn't love her, at least not enough, and I paid the price.

I turn on my e-reader and continue to read about my book boyfriend of the week, Jake Andrews. If only there were men like Jake Andrews in real life. A knock on the door pulls me from my book. I puff out a breath before calling out, "Yeah?"

The door opens, and in walks the man of the hour. Jack Kane, my father. I sit up on the bed, surprised.

"Hey, Summer," he says softly, his eyes bright.

"Hey, dad." I stand up and walk over to give him an extremely awkward one armed hug.

"You are so beautiful, baby girl," he says, shaking his head in awe.

"Thanks," I answer shyly. He looks the same. Tall, standing at about 6'1, with light brown hair and dark eyes, my father is one of those men who will always be handsome. He must be about forty five now, but apart from a few laugh lines, he looks younger than his age. He's wearing jeans, and a leather jacket over a black T-shirt. He probably rode his motorcycle here.

"You didn't wanna see me?" he asks, looking worried.

"Just wanted to settle in," I say, blushing. Trust my dad to get straight to the point.

"I didn't even see you last year for your birthday, Summer, it's been two years since I've seen my own daughter," he says, brows furrowing.

I shrug, because I have no idea what he expects me to say to that.

"How's Xander treating you?" he asks, thankfully changing the subject.

"He's wonderful," I say, a smile forming on my lips. My brother makes me feel welcome here, and I feel like I've known him my whole life.

"He loves you." I nod, giving him a forced smile. He tells me Xander loves me, but not him. Again, I have no idea what to say. He exhales, a look of regret and sadness flashing in his eyes.

"If you ever need *anything*, you come to me, okay?" he says, his dark brown eyes staring into mine.

I nod and force a smile. He scowls, and stares at me like he wants to say something else, but doesn't. He gives me a pained smile, and then leaves.

As soon as the door closes, I sag onto the bed, relieved. I didn't have a father my whole life, and I don't intend on having one now. Not that I don't love him, because I do. But it hurts, even after all these years.

Truth be told, I'm scared to let him in. He wasn't there for me, no matter how much I wished for it. I didn't want any money or gifts from him, I just wanted him. I wanted him to be there for my graduation, for my sports carnivals and dance recitals. I used to imagine him being there in the audience one day, watching me, but it never happened. He let me down each time, because he never came. That was the

25

hardest, starting to believe what my mother told me, that it was true - maybe he didn't want me.

After everything, it's just a little unnerving being in his presence. I still feel like that little girl who wants his attention. If Xander wasn't here, I wouldn't have come at all.

I wouldn't have felt that I was welcome.

CHAPTER THREE

The next day, I open the door, surprised to see Reid standing there. And that he actually knocked for once.

"You knocked," I say, stepping aside for him to enter.

"Yeah, well, it was locked for once." He grins at me. Oh, right.

I walk in front of him to the kitchen. "Xander's not here."

"Where did he go?" he asks, opening the fridge and helping himself to a bottle of water.

"Gym."

"Right, I'm heading there now so I'll catch up with him then," he says, his eyebrows scrunching together.

"Are you okay?" I ask.

"Yeah. How are you settling in?" he asks, looking like he genuinely wants to know.

"Great, actually. Feels like I've known Xander my entire life." I smile fondly, thinking about my brother.

"Yeah, he can't stop talking about you," Reid says, running his finger absently along his scarred jaw line.

"Do you maybe want to…" he trails off, staring at me.

"What?" I ask warily, when his gaze doesn't budge.

He clears his throat. "You look… beautiful today."

Wait, did he just say that? "Umm. Thank you," I reply, looking down at my frayed denim shorts and white singlet top. I glance up to see his eyes on my thighs.

"Reid," I say, smiling when he trails his gaze from my thighs to my face, his perusal bold. "Not one for subtlety, are you?"

He leans down onto the kitchen bench, his lip twitching. "I can't help it. It's been so long since I've seen something I wanted this bad."

"Umm," I mumble, the look on his face leaving me incoherent. I don't think any man has ever looked at me like that. Like he's dying of thirst and I'm the iced water. I shift on my feet under his scrutiny.

"You're not so bad yourself," I finally reply, leaning on the bench, so our elbows are almost touching.

He tilts his head, regarding me. "I told you… trouble."

I roll my eyes. "How so?"

"I'm standing here right now, watching you. Pretended I came here to see Xander, when I knew he was already gone, just so I could get a few minutes alone with you. I can't seem to stop thinking about you. Trouble."

My eyes widen in surprise. "You came here to see me?"

"I did, and now I can see it was a mistake. You're not for me, Summer, I shouldn't have come here," he says, pulling back to stand straight. His eyes are now shuttered, his expression closed off.

Having no idea what to say to that, I stay quiet.

"I gotta head to the gym," he says, turning his back on me and leaving.

*****

My first week living with Xander passes quickly. He goes to work, or goes to the gym with the guys. Most days they come here to hang out, and I cook us all dinner. They act like they haven't had a home cooked meal in years, and it feels good to be making myself useful in the house.

Reid doesn't come over as much as Dash and Ryan, and when he does, he's his usual charming self. We never mention him coming to see me. Sometimes I catch him staring at me when he thinks I'm not looking, but then his trademark scowl takes over, and then I think I imagined the moment we had when he came over altogether.

I glance down and look at the newspaper once more, hoping I missed something. There are hardly any jobs available for an unskilled worker like me. I was hoping for a waitressing job or something like that, any place that would take me on.

Giving up on the job ads, I decide to fill out my application for the course I want to do. After changing my mind several times, I've settled on nursing. I've heard it's a very competitive course to get into, but I have good high school grades, so hopefully it will be enough for me to gain entry to the

Tafe course. After that I can continue on to University, which is my plan.

"What are you doing?" Xander asks as he walks in, shirtless and sweaty. He went for a run about an hour ago. That must have been one long ass run.

"I was looking for a job, but nothing. So now I'm filling out the Tafe forms," I tell him, looking back down at the application.

"Why don't you ask Reid or Ryan for a job?" he says, shrugging like it's no big deal.

"Why would I ask them?"

"They own a bar. You could work there whenever you wanted, it'd be flexible for you with school, and there'd be people there to keep an eye on you," he says, lifting a brow.

"I didn't know they owned a bar," I grumble, not wanting to ask Reid for anything. "And why do I need someone to keep an eye on me?"

Xander shrugs. "Dad has a motorcycle shop you could work in, too. I work there a few days a week. And because you're beautiful, and new to town."

My eyes widen. That I did not know. Why did he seem so evasive about it before? "I'm sure I'll find something, and I don't need a babysitter."

"Stubborn." He chuckles. "The Kanes are all stubborn."

"Apparently."

"Yep, it's a fact," he says, smiling.

"I'm sure the Kanes are a lot of things," I say with a smirk.

"Yeah, all good things, of course."

I roll my eyes at him.

A knock on the door disturbs our banter, and Xander goes to answer it. As soon as he says the words 'hey, mum' I freeze. I don't want to meet his mother. I quickly stand and head towards my room. I'm halfway there, almost safe, when Xander calls out my name.

"Summer, come meet my mum," he says. I close my eyes for a second, before turning around. I try to smile but I think it comes out more like a grimace.

"Mum, this is Summer. Summer, this is my mum, Daria," he introduces. She is pretty, with mousy brown hair and clear blue eyes. She's a little on the thin side, and looks to be in her late forties or early fifties.

"Nice to meet you," I say, hoping they'll start to talk so I can sneak away. All I can think is, this is the woman my dad cheated with when he was married to my mother. I don't know how to feel. Daria's eyes seem kind as she watches me, before she finally speaks.

"Nice to meet you too, Summer, I've heard so much about you over the years."

"Really?" I manage to say, feeling surprised. I wouldn't have thought they would have discussed me at all. My eyes dart to my brother. He must see the look on my face because he frowns, and then starts to take Daria into the kitchen, offering her some coffee.

He glances back at me, so I attempt another smile before walking back into my room and quietly closing the door. She might have heard about me, but I've heard nothing about her except that she's a home wrecker.

31

Xander walks into my room an hour later without knocking. "What was that?" he asks, sounding confused, and a little angry.

"What was what?" I ask, closing my laptop.

"You looked at my mum like she was the devil," he says dryly.

"I don't know, I just don't know her," I lie.

"Summer, she's a nice person. She'll take care of you if you let her," he says, his voice gentling.

I can just imagine my mother turning in her grave right now.

"I don't need a replacement mother," I snap, losing my patience with the topic.

"Fuck, I know. I didn't mean that. You just looked upset, and..." he trails off, a look of realisation taking over his expression. "You're holding a grudge over something that happened what, nineteen years ago?"

"If dad didn't cheat with her, maybe I would have actually had a father growing up," I tell him, deciding to be honest. I know my feelings aren't fair. But that doesn't change the fact that I have them.

"So, you'd rather I wasn't born at all," he snaps back at me, making me wince. I didn't even think of that. In fact, I was just thinking of myself, no one else.

"Of course not, Xander," I say, rubbing my palm on my forehead.

He doesn't say anything, so I try again.

"I'll try next time, okay. I can't help how I feel, Xander, but I'll try," I promise him.

"Okay," he says, seemingly satisfied. We hear a knock on the door and Xander leaves to answer it.

I prop the pillows up, and lay back on them so I'm in a sitting position. Opening my laptop, I start to check my emails when Reid walks in. The door was left open, so he clearly didn't feel the need to knock. He's wearing basketball shorts, a tight white V neck T-shirt and sneakers.

"Hey," he says, a little warily.

"Hey."

"You okay?" he asks, looking concerned.

"I'm fine, why?" I ask. "You can sit down," I offer, pointing to the end of my bed. He hesitantly sits down, then looks back at me.

"Xander said you were upset about something," he says kindly. He sounds genuine, like he really cares about what I have to say.

"I'll be okay, I'm just trying to be a better person and not let my mother control or define my actions anymore," I say honestly. As it leaves my mouth, I can't believe I told him that. It's one of the most honest things I've ever said.

He nods, like he understands. "The fact that you're acknowledging it is a step in the right direction."

"I guess so. It's just messing with my mind right now," I admit.

"Trust me, I know the feeling," he says, scowling a little.

"I just don't want to hurt Xander. It's hard, though, when you grow up being told one thing, and then you find out it's not the truth at all."

33

"You're a good girl, Summer, forget about what you've been told. Start fresh and figure it out for yourself. Things aren't always what they seem," he says, looking down at the floor.

"You're being nice again, why?" I ask, closing my laptop.

He smirks. "Calling me out, are you?"

"Yeah, well, the hot and cold act is really getting old," I say, pursing my lips.

He nods twice. "Yeah, it would, wouldn't it? Look, I have a lot of shit going on in my life right now. I'm not in a good place. That doesn't mean I don't... care about you."

Then he stands up and walks away.

*****

"Get dressed, I'm taking you out." Xander says the next day when he walks into my room. "Dress in workout clothes," he adds before he closes the door.

'Out' ends up being me going with him to his gym. The gym is a warehouse, but it looks pretty decent. It has an octagon shaped cage, a boxing ring, and then a section with weights, a treadmill and other gym equipment.

I blink twice as I take in Ryan and Reid, boxing in the ring. They're both wearing nothing but basketball shorts and boxing gloves, oh my. I can't seem to tear my gaze from Reid, his body slick with sweat, his muscles rippling with every movement. I don't even know how I can tell which one Reid is from here, but I can. Reid purposely trips Ryan over, and I can hear them both laughing. They're obviously just messing around.

"What's with the weird shaped boxing ring?" I ask, curious.

Xander eyes me for a second before replying. "We like to fight."

"I can see that," I murmur, my eyes still locked onto Reid. I notice that Reid and Ryan have similar tattoos that start from their shoulder and finish above their elbows.

"Quit drooling, Sum.' Xander chuckles. I don't even bother denying it.

"Come on, this is women's porn right here," I tell him, swallowing hard when Reid throws off the gloves and runs his hand through his hair.

His impressive back is to me and I watch his muscles flex as he lifts his hands up behind his neck, talking with his brother.

"Ryan isn't the settling down type." He smirks. Who said I was checking out Ryan?

"And Reid?" I ask, trying to act casual.

Xander laughs, and I wince knowing this isn't going to be good. "Reid screws around less than Ryan. A lot less. He has a couple of fuck buddies he sticks to, but they know the deal. No commitment, no emotional attachment. He's cold, sis. Please tell me you're just asking out of curiosity, not interest."

I look at Xander and roll my eyes. "Of course I'm just curious. A man like that would eat me alive." And he would.

I hope.

Oh, hell.

"Good," Xander says, sounding relieved. "Come on, get on the treadmill."

"Are you hinting that you think I'm fat?" I gasp, just to annoy him.

Xander cringes, instantly backpedalling. "Of course not. You're perfect, but you still need to exercise. I thought we could teach you some self-defence, too."

"That actually sounds fun." I always wanted to learn self-defence. In the world we live in, every woman should know how to defend herself.

The twins walk down towards us. I stare at Reid. Seriously. Shorts slung so low I can see the sexy V of his hips. Tall, blonde, blue-eyed, he looks like a sexy Viking.

"What's she doing here?" Reid demands. Of course he has to open his mouth and ruin it.

"*She* is right here, and can talk for herself," I snap. His eyes connect with mine, and I can sense his irritation, and his... lust.

Shit.

"She's allowed to use the gym, Reid. It does belong to her father," Xander says calmly, slapping Ryan on the back in greeting as he walks towards the equipment.

"It does?" This is news to me. Reid's gaze softens slightly, probably feeling sorry for me because I know nothing about my own father.

I don't want or need his sympathy.

"Hey, Ryan," I greet, taking off my jacket, and putting it in the corner with my phone.

36

"Hey, Summer," he says, his eyes roaming over my black tights and tank top. They leave nothing to the imagination, even though most of my skin is covered, you can still see the shape of my figure. I suddenly feel a little self-conscious, so I walk in the direction Xander went. I can feel two matching sets of eyes on me as I walk away. Xander is on the phone, having a hushed conversation with someone, as I get on the treadmill and set it to a slow pace.

A very slow pace.

I used to dance in school, and that's the only form of exercise I'm really used to.

"Summer, I gotta go," Xander says, looking distracted.

"What? Why?"

"Jack rang, he needs me for something. I'll tell the twins to keep an eye on you," he says, kissing me on the forehead before leaving. He says something to Reid and Ryan, and to my dismay, Ryan leaves with him. They leave in a rush. I hope everything is alright. Reid walks over, looking put out that he has to babysit me.

The feeling is mutual.

"They had to go, so I'll take you home when you're done," he says, getting on the treadmill next to mine. Great, now I have to run right next to him. I layered on two sport bras hoping they would contain my breasts. Reid is about to have a first row seat to my DDs jiggling and bouncing as I jog. We exercise in silence for a few minutes, until I hear a soft groan escape Reid's mouth. I turn to look at him only to catch his eyes on my boobs.

CHANTAL FERNANDO

"Enjoying yourself?" I ask sweetly, laughing when he looks up sheepishly.

"You have nice tits," he says, shrugging.

"How romantic," I say dryly, crossing my arms over my chest.

"What? You were blessed in that department."

"Thanks... I think," I say, a flush working up my neck.

After twenty minutes I've had enough, and Reid sighs.

"Twenty minutes? That's how much stamina you have?"

"Depends on what I'm doing," I say with a grin.

Reid shakes his head, like he doesn't know what to do with me. I have a few ideas in mind I could share, if he's interested.

"Come on, I'll teach you a few moves." He gestures to the ring. I'm shocked when he grips me by the hips from behind, helping me up. Just a simple touch from him makes me shiver. I look down, not wanting him to see how he affects me. If he can make me feel like that with just one touch... Fuck.

He shows me a few different self-defence moves, and how to throw a punch. My heart races, and not just from the physical exertion.

"With all of us around you're going to be safe, but I guess it's good to know, right?" Reid says after he takes a sip from his water bottle. I stupidly didn't think to bring one, so he offers me his.

"Thanks." I take the bottle from him, our hands touching briefly in the exchange. I lift the bottle to my lips and drink, our eyes still connected. I hand him back the bottle and sit down on the mat.

"How old are you?" I ask him.

"Twenty-three."

I nod, he looks about that age. "Who's older?" I ask him.

"I am," he says, then drinks more water. I thought he would be older, even if it's just by minutes. Something about the way he can be so serious, whereas Ryan is carefree and easygoing.

"Thanks for staying with me, and for not being a dick," I say honestly, my eyes riveted on the smile that curves his lips.

"I have my moments."

I can't help smirking. "I'm glad."

"You liking it here?" he asks.

"I am."

"Anyone asked you out yet?"

"Nope."

"Probably don't know what to do with such beauty," he says softly.

I open my mouth, and then snap it shut. "What?" I whisper.

He shakes his head, as if clearing it. "You have to know how stunning you are."

I know I'm not completely unfortunate looking. I've been called pretty, and been noticed by men before. But no one has ever complimented me with such passion and intensity.

"You confuse me," I reply, averting my gaze.

He laughs humourlessly, sitting down next to me. "I can't even explain it. There's something about you."

We watch each other in silence for a few moments.

Reid clears his throat. "I should get you home."

"Okay," I say. But we don't move.

"Summer…" he trails off, staring at my lips. I move a little closer to him, and he moves the rest of the way so there is no space left between us.

"Are you going to kiss me?" I whisper, arrested in his blue gaze.

"I don't think that's a good idea," he whispers back, his eyes dropping to my mouth.

"Good ideas are overrated," I say breathily. I lick my lips, and his breath hitches.

He emits a low curse before capturing my lips with his, his hands in my hair. He licks at my mouth until I open for him, and then groans as he tastes me. When he starts to suck on my bottom lip, I shudder with pleasure. His hands move to my hips, but instead of pulling me closer, he pushes me away. He stands, turning his back to me and locking his fingers behind his neck. When he faces me again, his expression is once again shuttered. I puff out a sigh, and stand up, getting off the mat and walking towards the exit, picking up my jacket and phone on the way. I know exactly what he's going to say and I don't want to hear it.

He catches up to me and touches my elbow, steering me in the right direction. We walk in silence to his Jeep, and he opens the door for me to get in.

Reid turns the music on, but it doesn't dispel the tension surrounding us. Rihanna comes on, and I sing the lyrics to her song in my head as I stare out the window. My phone beeps with a text, and I giggle when I read it. It's from my friend back home about her new boyfriend.

Talk about TMI.

"Who's that?" Reid asks, being nosey.

"A friend," I reply, quickly texting her back saying that I really didn't need to know that.

"Who is he?" he asks, his voice tight.

"How's that any of your business? Just cos you don't want me doesn't mean others don't," I snap.

Reid curses, opening his mouth as if to say something, but then he closes it and stays quiet.

When we pull up to my house, I'm desperate to leave his presence.

Being rejected by him hurts.

"Do you have a key?" he asks in his deep sexy voice.

I nod. "Thanks for the ride," I say as I jump out, and walk swiftly to the house.

I don't look back, no matter how much I want to.

CHAPTER FOUR

I hop off Xander's motorcycle, adrenaline still pumping through my body. I've never ridden on a bike before, but wow, I'm definitely going to want to do that again. I take off my helmet and hand it over to Xander, along with his battered leather jacket and pull down at the hem of my red top which has ridden up past my belly button. I decided on this top with my favourite pair of skinny jeans, and my black knee high boots.

"You sure you don't wanna keep the jacket on?" Xander asks, not for the first time.

"You act like an old man, you know that?"

"I just got my sister, so I can't help it if I wanna protect you." He sticks his hands in his pockets.

"I get that, but I should be looking after you, baby bro," I tease.

He looks me over from head to toe. "You're what 5'4? I'm 6'2, I don't think anyone's going to believe you're older than me, Sum," he says, looking amused. "You're short and have a baby face."

"I'm 5'5," I huff.

Xander just laughs. "Besides, I don't wanna get into a fight when some asshole hits on you."

"Hey, I have needs, too," I joke, laughing when I see the look on his face.

"I'm going to pretend you never said that," he says, rubbing his temple as if to erase the image.

"Well, if some chick comes to hit on you, maybe I'm going to feel a little protective myself," I tell him.

He groans. "You mean you're going to be a cock block."

"Depends. Are you?" I ask, knowing I have him.

"We'll see." He shakes his head at me. He seems so much older than this age.

We walk into Reid's bar, and I take a look around. It's a smallish place, but it's packed out. There's a bar, tables, a few booth seats and a small dance floor. I can see Reid manning the bar, wearing a black shirt with the sleeves rolled up to his elbows. I quickly look away, not wanting to think of him right now. Dash calls us over when he sees us, sitting at a table with a cute looking redhead. He whispers something in her ear, and she frowns, but gets up and walks away.

"Hey, Dash," I say, taking a seat next to him.

"Don't you look gorgeous?" he says, his violet eyes gleaming in appreciation.

"Thank you," I say, wiggling my eyes at Xander, who scowls.

"What?" Dash asks, laughing.

I grin and wink at him, but don't reply. Xander gets us a round of drinks. I have a vodka sunrise, my favourite.

"You want me to ask the twins if they can give you a job?" Xander asks.

"No, I can ask myself," I say. I don't want my brother to have to talk for me. After not being able to find any jobs around, I decided I was going to have to suck up my pride and ask. I wait until the bar isn't busy and stand up, hoping to find Ryan.

There's no way in hell that I'm going to ask Reid.

Reid

Why the fuck is she here? My eyes must be popping out of my head right now. Summer just walked in, wearing a pair of jeans that I have to wonder how she managed to get on. They're like second skin, and riding so low on her hips I hope she doesn't need to bend over for anything. The thought of her bending over makes me instantly hard, and I cringe, discreetly adjusting myself.

I know Xander brought her here because this is a safe place for her, she can't get into any trouble with the amount of people that would protect her in here, but still.

I can't get that kiss out of my mind. She tasted so good, smelt so good.

It was perfect.

I'm not the man for Summer Kane, that much is true.

I turn around to get something out of the fridge, and when I turn back, there she is, standing right in front of me. Her lips are a shiny red, and my gaze can't help but be drawn to them, remembering how soft they were.

"Is Ryan here?" she asks, twirling a ring on her index finger. Of course she wants Ryan. She seems nervous, maybe she wants to ask him out after what happened between us. The thought makes me grip onto the side of the counter until my knuckles turn white. Why does it bother me so much? I have no fucking idea.

"He's back there," I tell her, gesturing to the office. "Go right in."

Fuck, I'm a bastard.

Summer

"Oh my god," I gasp in embarrassment, as I open the door to their office. Ryan is here alright. He's currently got a woman up against the wall. She's fully naked, and he has his jeans around his ankles. The man has a great ass, and it's in full view for me to see.

"Fuck," I hear him grunt as he sees me. He opens his mouth to say something, but I quickly turn around and leave before I can hear what he has to say. I don't look in Reid's direction as I walk back to our table.

"Everything okay?" Xander asks me.

"Fine," I huff.

"Then why are you blushing?" he asks, lifting up his beer and taking a long sip.

"Don't make me say it," I groan. Xander and Dash both sit forward, obviously not going to let this go.

"I went into the office to talk to Ryan, and let's just say, he's... busy," I say, rushing the words out. My face feels like it's on fire.

"Rookie mistake, Sum, never go into that office," he says, chuckling.

"I'll definitely remember that." Lesson learnt. Why did Reid send me there? He must have wanted to embarrass me, and he sure as hell succeeded.

"Don't be embarrassed," Dash drawls, pulling me in closer to him. I relax my shoulders and try to forget what I just witnessed, which is hard to do when Ryan walks over about twenty minutes later and sits next to me.

"Like what you saw?" he asks, wiggling his eyebrows. He doesn't seem that embarrassed, which makes it just a little more bearable.

"I think your technique could improve," I quip, smiling when everyone bursts into laughter.

"Is that right?" he drawls, smiling. He doesn't even get offended, which means he must be a stallion in bed.

"Definitely, maybe you should practice some more," I say, pursing my lips together to try and keep a serious face.

"That's a great idea. You wanna dance?" he asks me. I shrug, why not? When I stand he chuckles, and I can tell he thought I would turn him down. I did just catch him screwing another woman, but I have no interest in Ryan other than friendship.

"Look after her," Xander calls out, but I can see his attention is on a girl sitting in the corner.

I walk to the small, crowded dance floor, and Ryan pulls me closer, making a grinding motion with his hips. When he adds in a thrusting move, I burst out laughing.

"See, I can practise right here on the dance floor," he says, leaning closer so I can hear him. He smells like cologne and sex, and I wrinkle my nose at him. He smiles and puts his hands on my hips, as I swivel them seductively. He doesn't come too close, or move his hands anywhere inappropriate. This is just us dancing as friends, and I find myself having fun.

Ryan spins me around, and we're both laughing by the end of the song. We're walking back to the table when I see Reid staring daggers at me. Then he turns, looking around the bar until his eyes come across a stunning blonde. He waits until her eyes meet his, then tilts his head slightly towards the office. She smiles seductively, and walks towards the office, her hips shaking with each step. She opens the office door and walks in, Reid following her, and closing the door behind him. Ryan heads to the bar, taking over.

I swallow and look away, taking my seat at the table. I skull the rest of my drink, not even wanting to contemplate why I'm reacting the way I am. Reid and I are nothing, not even friends. I don't know how much time passes, but I distract myself with talking to Dash, Ryan and Xander, and having a few more drinks. The bar empties, so Ryan sits with me at the table.

When someone stands at the table, I can tell it's him without even having to look up. It's like he has some sort of pull over me, some sort of energy that attracts me.

I can feel him, without even touching him.

Ryan laughs at his brother. "'Bout time you got some action brother."

I swallow hard, still not looking up at Reid, waiting for him to leave.

Needing him to leave.

But he still stands there. I look at my brother instead, smiling shyly across the room at the mysterious girl.

"Summer."

Why can't he just leave? Now he wants to talk?

"Yeah?" I say, reluctantly looking up at him. He looks angry, for some reason. Like it was me that just screwed some random person in the office, like we didn't share that kiss.

"Did you ask Ryan whatever you needed to?" he asks with a smirk.

I look at Ryan. "Oh, right. I was wondering if you had any job openings?"

Reid looks surprised for a moment, but I don't have it in me to care why right now.

"Sure, you can work in the bar," Ryan offers, giving me a smile. Ryan is so easy to be around, I'll be glad to have him as my boss. Reid, on the other hand…

He watches me carefully, as if looking for a reaction from his little office romp. But he isn't going to get it. My body reacts to Reid, that much is certain, but I'm not one to play these games. I may not have that much experience, but I know I deserve better than this.

I ignore Reid for the rest of the night, but I can feel him watching me. I'm doing a shot with Ryan and Dash when Xander walks over, looking sheepish. He rubs his jaw, looking at me.

"What?" I ask him warily, rubbing the alcohol off my bottom lip.

"I'm not coming home tonight. Ryan or Reid will take you home," he announces. I look behind him to see the girl he was watching earlier. I decide not to make this easy on him. What are big sisters for, right?

"So, where are you going then?"

"To her house," he answers, his eyes narrowing.

"Do you even know her?"

"Summer…"

I cut him off. "What if she takes advantage of you?" I say it louder than necessary. The guys burst out in laughter, and Xander just shakes his head at me, amused.

"That's the plan, sis," he smirks.

"Hey!" I call out to the girl. She looks at me, looking a little frightened.

"No glove, no love," I remind her. Xander instantly grabs her hand and pulls her away, saving her from me.

"They grow up so fast," I muse, earning more laughter from the peanut gallery. Reid walks up to me, leaning on the bar facing me.

"We need to talk," he says, crossing his arms over his chest.

"We don't need to do anything," I return, looking at the dance floor which is suddenly very interesting.

"Summer, we can't just…"

"Can you call me a cab?" I ask him, interrupting his speech.

"I'm taking you home," he says, sounding irritated.

"Where's Ryan?" I ask, looking around. I swear he was here a second ago. When I see him heading to the

49

CHANTAL FERNANDO

office with a different chick, I gape. Again? Really? Reid chuckles at the look on my face and I hate that the sound sends shivers up my spine. I wobble a little, feeling tipsy.

"Give me thirty minutes and I'll take you home," he says, his tone final.

"I hope someone disinfects the surfaces in that office," I say, more to myself than him.

"Well, when you start working maybe that can be your duty," he says dryly, a scowl etched on his face.

"If I'm cleaning it, I get to use it, too," I say, looking up at him.

He's so handsome it hurts.

"I'm sorry, what?" he growls.

I shrug, as if I don't care either way.

"You think you can take some guy, fuck him in there and then I'll let him live?" he says with a humourless chuckle.

"Don't think it's any of your business," I say.

He smiles evilly. "Xander, Dash, Ryan, your father... Do I need to keep going? There's no way any man you decide to get with will survive the night."

"Why do you care so much?" I snap at him.

"That's the question of the hour, isn't it?" he says dryly.

"I don't get you!" I say, frustrated. I head for the dance floor and stay there for a few more songs. When I return to the bar, I walk up to Reid and say, "I need another drink. Want one?"

Reid is about to reply when he looks towards the entrance. I lean to the right to see what he's looking at, gaping when I see it's my father. I flop down on the bar stool. My father is kissing a woman. Or maybe I should say a girl, because she looks no more than twenty five. I grimace, turning away from him, and ask Ryan for another shot.

Ryan grins and pours me two. What a legend. I down one shot, frowning when Reid takes the other away from me.

"I'm cutting her off, Ryan," he tells his brother. Ryan gives me a sympathetic glance, leaning over and patting me on the head.

"Ry, stay with her here for a sec," he says, walking off towards Jack. He says something to him, and then my dad glances towards me, looking surprised to see me here. He says something to his girl and she nods slightly, sending a glare my way before walking to a table filled with girls. I look away, and concentrate on Ryan instead.

"How was your second go?" I blurt out.

He chuckles. "Better than the first."

"Really?" I ask, a vision of his sexy ass coming to mind. I wonder if Reid's looks the same. No, probably sexier.

Ryan bursts out laughing. "What were you just thinking about?"

"Nothing," I say quickly. "When do I start work?"

"You can come in tomorrow, alright. We actually do need someone. As you can see it's just Reid and me here tonight. We have another guy who works here, but today's his off day," he explains.

"Interesting," I muse. Ryan laughs, putting his arm around me and pulling me close.

"Jack's coming over," he says. I notice a lock of his hair out of place, so I lift my hand up and fix it.

"Good for him," I say dryly.

"Hey, don't be judgemental," he says softly. Is that what I was being?

"Summer, I didn't expect to see you here," my dad says, coming and standing next to me.

"Well, here I am," I say in a fake cheerful tone.

"Nice to see you again, sweetheart." He sounds like he really means it.

"Where did Reid go?" I ask him, looking around.

"Why?" His eyes suddenly turn hard.

"Cos he's taking me home," I say, tilting my head. Why the questions?

"I can take you home," he offers.

"No, thanks," I politely decline, looking around for Reid, desperate to get away from the man in front of me. When I see him in a heated argument with a petite girl with short blonde hair, I change my mind. I wait until my dad is busy looking at the girl he came in with, then I walk outside and call a cab, which luckily arrives a few minutes later. I almost fall asleep on the drive home, but manage to stay awake. I pay the cab driver, and hop out, walking quickly to my front door. I unlock the door, which takes a few tries, and lock it behind me as soon as I enter. I undress and walk to my room, not caring right now where my clothes land. Tying my hair out of my face, I get up on my knees on my bed, and face plant into the mattress. Sighing in contentment, I finally let myself fall asleep.

CHAPTER
FIVE

Summer

I flop over onto my stomach, and groan. I can hear someone banging on the door. Why? Why me? My throat is parched and my eyes won't open. I put the pillow over my head to block out the banging, but it doesn't stop. I will myself out of bed, throwing on an oversized T shirt, and tripping over my handbag on the way to the front door. I look through the peep hole, only to see Reid standing there. Unlocking the door, I pull it open and come face to face with an extremely pissed off alpha male.

"What?" I ask grumpily, not waiting for his answer as I turn to head back to bed. Surely he has a key? He's over here all the damn time.

"Where the fuck did you go last night?" he booms. I wince as my head throbs.

"I caught a cab home," I say, rubbing my eyes.

"You caught a..." he trails off, laughing humourlessly. "Next time tell someone where you're fucking going so we don't have to spend the night worried about you," he growls, walking to the fridge and helping himself to some orange juice.

"Why didn't you just come here to see if I was home?" I ask.

"Of course I fucking did that! No one answered the door and there were no lights on," he practically growls at me, and if looks could kill I would surely be dead right now.

"Can you please yell at me later? I'm hung over and I have the worst headache," I sulk. His expression softens a little at what I assume is my pathetic appearance.

"Go to bed," he says. I don't need to be told twice. I'm warm under the covers when he walks into the room holding a drink, and two pain killers.

"Thank you," I tell him gratefully, swallowing the tablets with some orange juice. I'm surprised at his thoughtfulness.

I yawn and offer him a smile. "Is Xander still out?"

"Yup," he says, popping the p.

I frown. "I should call him."

"You should let your brother be," he says flippantly, sitting down on my bed.

"Where's the fun in that?" I say, my lips curving.

"I almost got into it with Jack last night." He's staring at my stuffed unicorn on my shelf, not looking at me.

"What happened?" I ask, raising my head.

"Just an argument."

"How do you know Jack?" I ask him.

Reid collapses on my bed next to me and stares at the roof. "He used to be friends with... my dad."

"Where's your dad now?" I ask him softly, hoping he hadn't passed away.

"In jail," he huffs, and I can feel the anger lurking behind his words. I think he expects me to pry, and ask why he's in jail, so I don't.

"Okay," I whisper, leaving it at that.

"Why did you leave? I told you I was going to take you home," he says, biting out each word.

"You were busy talking to some chick, and I just wanted to get away from my dad, so I left," I admit. I didn't want to bring up the girl because I didn't want him to think I was jealous. There's clearly nothing between us, especially after what he did last night. We're just friends, and I suppose I could always use more of those. Truth be told, I like being around Reid. Sure, he may be surly and brooding sometimes - okay, most of the time - but he has this quality about him that I can't help but be drawn to.

"About last night..." he starts, but doesn't say anything else.

"You don't need to explain anything, Reid," I say softly, my eyelids feeling heavy.

"Why haven't you asked me about my scar?" he asks, changing the subject.

I shrug. "I don't even notice it anymore," I say, meaning every word.

It's a part of him, and it's neither ugly, nor beautiful, it's just him.

*****

I wake up suddenly, sitting up in bed. I almost squeal when I see a blond head poking out of my leopard print sheets.

Reid is in my bed, fast asleep.

He looks so huge in my bed and he's taking up a good three quarters of the space.

I lean over him, smiling to myself. He looks so peaceful and serene, I don't want to wake him, so I quietly leave the room, heading straight for the shower. I take my time in there, dry myself and then stand naked in front of the mirror staring at my reflection. I've definitely seen better days. I grab a makeup wipe to remove the black under my eyes from my mascara, and put moisturizer on my face.

"Yep, this is as good as it's going to get today," I mutter to myself, throwing on my pink fluffy robe. I open the bathroom door and walk out, the steam escaping the room with my exit. I take two steps down the hall before I face plant into a rock hard wall of muscle.

Reid Knox, shirtless.

I swoon.

His arms instantly come around me to stop me from falling over, and my face rests against his chest, his scent engulfing me.

"Morning," I mumble into his chest. His body shakes with silent laughter.

"Morning," he says huskily, as he steps back so our bodies are no longer touching.

"You slept in my bed," I point out.

"I did," he says, suddenly frowning.

"What is it?" I ask, curious at the flash of confusion I see in his eyes.

He clears his throat and shrugs his shoulders a little. "It's nothing."

"Yeah, I'm going to need a little more than that." I cross my arms over my chest, staring him down.

Reid scowls. "Can I go to the bathroom without being asked a million questions? Fucking Spanish inquisition."

"Okaaaay, then," I drawl, stepping around him and storming to my room. I lock the door behind me, letting my robe fall to the floor. I put on a pair of red panties and a matching bra, followed by some distressed light denim jeans and a white V neck top. Shoving my feet into my fluffy pink Ugg boots, I open my door and walk into the kitchen. I'm in the middle of frying some eggs and bacon when Xander walks in, gracing me with a huge smile when he sees I'm making breakfast.

"What? Your woman doesn't feed you?" I ask, raising an eyebrow. Xander sits down at the breakfast bar and eyes the frying pan.

"Why would she have to? I knew I had my own little chef at home," he teases, pulling off his shirt and throwing it on the counter.

"How was your night?" I ask, making a face when I realize what I asked. Xander laughs, looking amused. Reid walks out, freshly showered and wearing nothing but his jeans, which aren't even buttoned. They're riding so low on his hips that I can see he's going commando from here, and the thin trail of blonde hair from below his navel, disappearing into his jeans is enticing enough to lick.

"What are you doing here?" Xander asks, standing up and eyeing Reid.

"Who do you think kept an eye on your sis when you bailed last night?" Reid says, his narrowed eyes showing his unhappiness.

"Sit down, both of you," I command, serving three plates. I take my own to the couch and turn on the TV. Moments later they both join me. We all eat in silence, and I watch as the boys both polish their entire plates in minutes.

"There's more in the pan," I tell them, laughing when they both instantly get up to load their plates with second servings. The tension now broken, we all chat as we watch music videos.

"Ryan told me to come into work today, I think," I tell Reid. I was a little drunk, but I'm pretty sure he told me to.

"I'll take you in, I gotta drop by anyway," he offers, which I think is sweet.

"What the fuck is going on between you two?" Xander blurts out, looking curious rather than angry.

"Nothing," I say incredulously, turning to look at Reid, who remains quiet.

"What's your issue, Xander?" Reid asks him, the atmosphere thickening.

"Reid, let's go," I say, grabbing my bag and heading towards the door. I walk out the front, and leave them to say whatever they need to. I feel like this whole thing has nothing to do with me. I lean against Reid's Jeep, waiting for him. He walks out about ten minutes later, and opens the door for me. He rounds the car and slides into the driver's seat and slams the door shut. He doesn't say anything for the entirety of the journey, but I can feel his mind at work as he mulls over his thoughts. I choose to stay blissfully ignorant, looking out the window and pretending I can't feel the tension in the car.

"Ry's not here yet," Reid says as he pulls into the car park.

"Who's here, then?" I ask, seeing that the bar is open.

"Tag."

"Tag?" I repeat, my eyes widening when I see a sexy guy walk out of the bar, lighting up a smoke. He has a shaved head, and a hot body, dressed in a wife beater, dark denim jeans and black motorcycle boots.

Reid stares at me and scowls. "He has a different bitch every night, don't even think about it."

"That's Tag?" I ask, wide eyed. And I'm working with this man?

Perhaps I should pay them.

I didn't realize I had said this out loud until Reid curses and gets out of the car, slamming the door shut. I get out of my side and storm over to him.

"And don't call me a bitch," I snap.

"When did I fucking call you a bitch?" he asks, looking confounded.

"You called women bitches, and if you haven't noticed, I'm a woman, and I don't fucking appreciate being called a bitch!" I sneer at him.

"Oh, trust me, I know you're all woman," he says in a smooth tone, staring at my breasts and then my hips.

"That was a seedy look," I lie. Really, it was hot and smouldering. Reid chuckles, like he knows what I'm thinking.

"The way your body reacts to me, beauty, I'm pretty sure that's not what you think. You're going to be so responsive, I can hardly wait for a taste," he says softly so only I can hear.

"Yeah, trust me, that's not going to happen, especially after last night," I snap, crossing the road without him. Tag's brows furrow as he watches me.

"Hey, Tag," I say, smiling widely at him.

"Tag, you don't get to touch this one," Reid says from behind me, smirking.

Tag chuckles huskily, pulling out another cigarette from the packet. "There's a first for everything, I guess."

"You're... hot," I blurt out. Reid shifts on his feet, taking me by the arm and pulling me inside. "You even look at him and I'll fire him. He has a kid, you want that on your conscience?"

"You're a dick," I tell him, looking around the bar.

"Summer, I didn't fuck that girl last night, so retract your claws," he whispers into my ear. He didn't? This man is so damn confusing. I can't help but feel relief, but when you look at it, does it really change anything between us?

"So what did you do, then? Play Monopoly?" I say sarcastically. I purse my lips waiting for his answer.

"She started to kiss me and I pushed her away. I couldn't go through with it, it wasn't her I wanted."

"So, kissing means nothing to you? Maybe I should go and kiss the next guy that walks by and see how you like it?"

"If you want to see a fight, sure," he says, narrowing his eyes a little.

"Hypocritical bastard," I mutter, gritting my teeth. Why do I like him again?

"Look at me, hey," he says, holding my chin in his palm. "I shouldn't want you. I'm not good enough for you. I know it and you know it. But that doesn't stop me from wanting you. Just being near you... You bring me peace, beauty," he says in a soft unwavering tone, briefly resting his forehead against mine. I stand there in shock.

Speechless.

Reid heads behind the bar, leaving me standing there, gaping like a goldfish. Ryan walks into the bar, saving me.

"Hey, Sum, you remembered," he says, tugging at a lock of my hair.

"Of course I did. What kind of employee would I be if I didn't show up my first day of work?" I ask in a saccharine sweet tone.

"Probably like the employees I'm used to," he says, chuckling. He bounces on his feet, full of energy.

"It's just the three of you?" I ask, looking around. There are about five customers, three of them sitting alone and staring into their drinks. Must be drowning their sorrows, because it's only two pm.

"Yeah, we had another girl, but as of last month she quit," he says, his eyes darting towards Reid. Or was it Tag?

"Which one of them chased her off?" I ask, dying to know.

"Work gossip another day." He chuckles. "Today, let me show you the ropes. You ever worked at a bar before?"

"Not exactly," I admit, but how hard could it be?

*****

Four hours and two broken glasses later, I'm getting used to everything. There's a chart telling me exactly what to put in each drink, and Reid showed me how to use the cash register. A customer told me I wasn't very good at pouring beer, but apart from that, I think I'm doing pretty well. Tag went home, leaving me alone with the twins.

"Can I help you?" I ask the next customer, cringing when I see it's the woman my dad was with here last night.

"Vodka orange," she purrs, a smug smile on her face. What the hell does she have to be smug about? So, you're fucking my dad, congratu- fucking- lations.

"So, you're Jack's kid," she says, handing me a fifty. I wonder if this is my dad's money she's using.

Probably.

I don't answer her, because I have nothing to say.

"I didn't even know he had a daughter until last night," she says, searching my face for a reaction. I school my expression, not wanting her to know that her comment stung, because it did.

"Are you going to be my new mommy?" I ask sarcastically, handing her the change.

"You're not going to get in the way of Jack and me," she sneers, her face turning red with the hatred in her expression. She storms off, back to her table where her minions sit.

"You okay?" Reid asks, coming up behind me.

"Why would she think I'd get in the way of her and dad? What the fuck?"

"She knows Jack loves you, it's easy for anyone to see, Summer," he tells me, grabbing my hand and rubbing my knuckles with his thumb.

"Jack could care less about me," I say, walking towards the end of the counter where a customer stands. I serve him his drink, and then watch as another familiar face walks up to me. The blonde haired girl from last night. I remember Reid was talking to her just before I left. Apparently the same people come here every day. Great, just great.

I'm about to ask what can I get for her when Reid walks up to me. "I'll serve her. You go ask Ry if he needs you to do anything," he says, waiting for me to leave before he says another word.

What the hell?

Who is this woman?

I find Ryan in the office, actually doing work instead of his usual activities in here.

"Need me to do anything else, Ryan?" I ask him, walking in and plopping down on his desk.

"If you can write down your availability that would be great," he says, pressing buttons on his calculator.

"Does Reid have a girlfriend?" I ask, not looking him in the eye as I say it.

"Nope. Why? You interested in the position?" he asks, chuckling like it's hilarious. And what if I was?

At my silence, Ryan lifts his head to look at me, the smile falling off his face as he realizes why I'm asking.

I'm interested.

In fact, I'm already a little invested.

Ryan stares at me for a second. "Reid is my brother and I love him. He's a great guy, but he's also very complicated. I'm not sure if you should head down that road with him, Sum. Especially with your dad and Xander, and yeah, I don't think it's the best idea."

"And if I decided not to heed your warning?" I ask him, tapping my foot on the floor.

"I support Reid with anything he chooses to do, but I'm also most probably going to say I told you so in the end." He offers me a sad smile, and then looks back down at his work.

"Where's your mum?" I ask him.

"Dead," he answers, his expression darkening.

"I'm sorry," I whisper. I've always been awkward in these moments, having no idea what to say or to offer comfort. I shift on the desk.

"Its fine, Summer," Ryan says, his lip twitching at my obvious discomfort. I pick up a piece of paper and pen and write down the hours I can work, which happen to be twenty four seven until two months' time when my course starts.

"Here," I tell him, handing him the piece of paper. He quickly scans it and grins. "So we have you all day, every day, for two whole months, huh?"

"Yup."

"Perfect, cos this Thursday Reid and I have somewhere we need to be, so you and Tag can man the bar," he says.

"Alright," I say, dying to ask where they need to be but refraining.

"Where's Reid?" he asks, handing me another paper asking me for my bank details.

"Serving customers at the bar," I sulk.

Ryan chuckles. "Who's there? Rachel or Kyra? Or Tegan?"

I turn my head to glare at Ryan. "What the hell, Ryan?"

"What? You're a nice girl and…"

"Ryan," Reid seethes, walking in and glaring at his brother. They have a silent conversation, until finally Ryan sighs, obviously giving in.

"Summer, watch the bar for a sec," Reid says, dismissing me. His eyes are still on his brother. I jump up off the table and walk out, making sure not to touch Reid as I exit. I close the door behind me and stand in from of the cash register. There are no customers waiting to be served, so I just wipe down the table, wondering what the hell those two could be talking about. A shiver runs down my spine alerting me that Reid is behind me.

"You okay?" he rumbles, his body close but not touching mine.

"Fine," I huff, looking around for something else to clean.

"Summer…"

"Who is that girl?" I ask, cutting him off. I sound like a jealous wife but seriously, I know that everyone is keeping things from me. I just want to know why, or in this case who.

"Don't worry about her, Summer," he says in a bored tone, and I can tell it annoys him that I'm questioning him, demanding answers. Well, too freaking bad.

"What's her name?" I ask, spinning to face him.

"I don't belong to you, Summer," he says, putting me in my place.

I swallow hard, having a hard time maintaining eye contact with his intense gaze. "You're right."

I step away and around him, walking back into the office. "Hey Ryan, do you still need me?"

"No babe, you can go. Tag will be back here in about twenty minutes anyway. I'm about to head out, too," he says, stacking papers into a neat pile.

"Can you give me a lift home?" I ask him, shifting on my feet. He gives me a curious look before nodding.

"Of course I can. You know I can never turn down a pretty face." He smirks.

"Trust me, I know," I mutter, earning me a chuckle from the man in question.

"I'll meet you at your car." I walk out of the bar without glancing at Reid, although I can feel his eyes on me. I stand in the car park, suddenly realising I have no idea which car Ryan drives. I've seen him driving Reid's Jeep but obviously he didn't come in that today because Reid did.

When Ryan walks out holding two helmets, a slow smile spreads on my lips. I could almost do a happy dance, that's how much I love being on the back of a bike.

"I didn't know you had a bike," I say as he puts the helmet on me.

"We all have bikes, babe," he says, shaking his head at me.

Reid has a motorcycle?

"Yes, Reid has one. It's a beast of a bike, too," Ryan says.

Did I say that aloud?

"Your face shows everything you're thinking, Summer," he says, that perpetual grin on his smug face.

I roll my eyes and jump on.

CHAPTER SIX

Reid is absent for the next few days, working different shifts than me. Every time our paths do manage to cross, I try not to look at him, which is harder than I thought it would be.

Thursday rolls around, and Tag and I are alone in the bar from six pm until closing, which can be anywhere from midnight til three am, depending on how many customers we have. I'm making a cocktail when I see Reid walk in, looking agitated. His eyes shift as he looks around the bar, before he stares straight at me. He shakes his head slightly from side to side, as if to clear it, and then heads into the back. He comes out moments later with Ryan, who is also acting a little off. Ryan approaches me and offers me a smile that doesn't reach his ocean blue eyes.

"We're off. If Tag wants to close early, that's fine. Also don't go anywhere alone, alright?" he says, placing his hand on my shoulder.

"Okay. Is everything alright?" I ask, worried. Something feels off.

"Its fine, don't worry. Tag is going to keep an eye on you." He places a chaste kiss on my temple. I look back at Reid who is standing at the door watching us.

I look down when it looks like he's just going to leave without saying a word.

It really hurts.

The night goes slow as ever, even working with Tag, which is usually a heap of fun. Reid is right about Tag and women, he makes even Ryan look good. A man walks up to the bar and waits for me to serve him.

"What can I get you?" I ask him.

"You can give me your name, for a start," he says, leering at me. Working at a bar, being hit on is kind of expected. But I still don't really like or welcome it. Some men can take for no for an answer, but others...

"What can I get you to drink?" I ask again, emphasizing the drink part. I'm not on the menu, and neither is my name or any other knowledge about me.

"I'm surprised you're not there with them," he sneers, his face scrunching.

"What?" I ask, completely confused.

"What, aren't you one of Reid's bitches? I know how they all like to hang around after and wait for him," he says, staring at me accusingly. Ignoring the douche bag, I walk over to Tag and stand next to him.

"Problem?" he asks, instantly scanning the bar. When he sees the man that spoke to me he walks over. I start to serve another customer, waiting for Tag to come back so I can ask him what the hell is going on.

The man leaves and Tag returns, but he ignores me. I corner him when all the customers are gone.

"Explain," I demand, crossing my arms over my chest.

"Not my place, Summer," he says.

I don't say anything.

"You wanna head home early? I'm going to close up now," he says, avoiding looking at me.

My nails dig into my palms. I inhale and exhale, trying to calm myself down.

Everyone knows what's going on except for me.

And these people are meant to be my friends and family.

"Yeah, I'll go," I say quietly, getting my handbag.

"Straight home, Summer," he says. "Wait, I'll walk you out."

I nod my head.

*****

I can hear banging on the front door, followed by the sound of masculine voices.

"Don't fucking start, Xander," I hear Reid snap. Reid? What's he doing here?

I sit up in bed and watch as my bedroom door opens and Reid walks in.

"What are you doing here?" I ask, my voice thick with sleep. He remains silent, taking off his shoes and his T-shirt. When he lifts up the covers and slides into bed next to me, my mouth is hanging open so wide I'm sure he'd get ideas if he was able to see it.

"What do you think you're doing?" I grate out, pissed at his audacity.

71

"I need you," he says quietly, his voice sounding hoarse. He pulls me closer to him, and cocoons me in his warmth. Why was I angry at him again?

"I don't like you," I mumble, as I dose off back to sleep.

*****

I wake up with a hand on my ass, squeezing one of the globes. I lean into Reid's touch, moaning when his hands move to cup both of my breasts. Reid's satisfied chuckle pulls me out of the moment, making me remember exactly what's going on right now. I pull away and sit up, gasping when I take in his face.

"What happened?" I ask taking in his cut lip, and bruised eye.

"Got into a fight," he says, shrugging his shoulder. When he grimaces at the movement, I know he's probably been hit in the ribs.

"With who?" I demand.

"Don't worry about it, Summer," he says softly, taking my arm and trying to pull me closer.

"So what, you think you can ignore me for as long as you want, and then just come over and hop into my bed?" I snap, getting out of the bed and looking around for some pants. I'm dressed in just an oversized top and panties.

Not even sexy panties at that.

"Beauty." He sighs, running his hands through his messy hair. I see my pink track pants thrown over my chest of drawers and grab them, shoving them on angrily.

"I don't get you, Reid, either you want me or you don't. And if you don't, that's fine. Just let me go so I can find someone who does!" I yell, my anger over the last few days erupting.

"Does this look like I don't want you?" he says dryly, moving the sheet aside so I can see his straining erection.

Holy shit, he is huge.

I open my mouth. And then close it. And then open it again.

"Don't try to distract me with that thing!" I yell, pointing at it accusingly.

"Summer, you don't understand…"

"You're right, I don't. If you think your morning wood is supposed to be a compliment, you're mistaken," I growl.

Reid's lips tighten, and for a moment I think he wants to laugh at me.

I am so in over my head with him.

He makes me stupid.

He makes me forget myself.

He makes me want him more than my own sanity.

"Where were you last night?" I ask, enunciating each word. He rubs his face, not even wincing when he touches his injuries.

When he doesn't reply, I walk out of the room and head for a shower. When I return to the room thirty minutes later, Reid isn't there.

CHAPTER SEVEN

"Dinner's ready!" I call out to the guys, who are playing video games and drinking beer.

"Smells good, sis," Xander says as he walks up, kissing me on the top of my head.

"Of course it does," I brag, placing all the plates on the dining table. Dash and Ryan walk over, taking a seat, serving their plates and digging in. I look at the spare seat that would be occupied by Reid if he was here. It had been two days since I saw him last.

"Seriously, this is the best steak I've ever had," Ryan says as he takes a huge bite. I take a bite of mashed potatoes and wonder where the hell Reid is.

"I'm moving in," Dash says, his mouth full.

"Where's Reid?" I blurt out, not being able to hold it in any longer.

The table goes silent.

Ryan keeps his gaze trained on his food when he says, "He's at home."

"Why didn't he come over for dinner?" I ask, noticing Xander frowning from the corner of my eye.

"He has company," Ryan says reluctantly, finally lifting his head to look at me.

"I see," I mumble, now looking down at my own plate. That's Ryan's nice way of saying Reid is at home, screwing another woman.

Fuck. This.

Xander gets up and heads into the kitchen, walking back and putting a drink on the table next to my plate.

"Thanks," I tell him as I open the cap and skull it. It's one of those girly vodka mixed drinks that Ryan bought for me since he knows I don't care much for beer.

"Dad says he wants you to go over to his house tomorrow for dinner," Xander announces to the table.

"Why didn't he tell me himself?" I ask.

"He said you wouldn't answer your phone," he says, eyeing me knowingly.

Oh yeah.

"I'm not sitting there with him and that bitch," I say bitterly, finishing my last bite.

"What?" my brother asks, sitting up straight in his chair.

"She came up to me and said some shit. I can't stand her, and frankly I'm not too fond of Jack either," I say, looking down.

"Summer…"

"Can we go out?" I ask, standing up and clearing mine and Ryan's plates. I don't wait for an answer because I'm going out with or without them. I walk into my room, closing the door behind me with a push of my foot. Knowing exactly what I'm going to wear, I strip off my top and unbutton my jeans. I'm about to push the jeans off when Ryan walks in without knocking. I squeal a little, covering my bra clad breasts with my hands. Instead of being embarrassed, Ryan grins and closes the door behind him.

"You have a smoking body, Summer," he says, approval dripping from his tone.

"I'm glad you approve," I say dryly, opening my wardrobe and pulling out my little black dress. Or should I say *the* little black dress.

There is little this dress *can't* do.

"Are you alright?" he asks, taking a seat on my bed.

"Are you just going to sit there and watch me undress?" I ask as I let my hands drop from my breasts so he has a plain view of my bra.

"Hold on a sec," he says as he lifts his phone to his ear. "Hey, bro."

My heart stops beating.

"Just wanted to see where you are tonight cos I'm taking Sum out and I don't want her to run into you," he says into the phone, smirking at whatever Reid replies . Ryan stares up at me, a mischievous look taking over his face.

"You can take the bra off, too, Summer, nothing I haven't seen before, trust me," he says, I'm sure so that Reid can hear. I roll my eyes at his antics and take my dress into the bathroom so I can undress in peace.

I exit the bathroom twenty minutes later, dolled up and ready to party. With my black dress, I'm wearing my strappy platform heels that make my legs look longer than they really are. My brown hair is down and ironed dead straight, and my makeup consists of a brown smokey eye and a nude lip.

"Someone's dressed to kill," Ryan says as I walk back into my room, doing a little turn to show him the back of my dress, or lack thereof. He stands up and walks over to me.

"You look beautiful. My brother's a dumbass," he says, checking me out again.

"Thank you," I tell him, meaning it. That was the perfect thing to say. I walk out, frowning when I see Xander and Dash missing in action.

"They had to go somewhere, they'll meet us out. Come on," he says, heading to the front door. I lock up the house and slide into his car, wrinkling my nose.

"This car smells like… sex," I say, looking at Ryan's profile. Ryan laughs but doesn't explain. Knowing him, he probably got some action before he came for dinner.

"How come I've never seen Dash hook up?" I ask, suddenly curious.

Ryan shrugs, keeping his eyes on the road. "That's Dash's story."

I make a growling sound in my throat and Ryan laughs. "So glad to amuse," I deadpan. When we pull up into a car park of an apartment complex my head snaps to Ryan.

"What the f…"

"I have to stop by and get dressed, I'm not going out like this," he says gesturing to his jeans and T-shirt. He looks fine to me.

"Fine, go on, I'll wait here," I say, pulling out my phone from my handbag to keep me amused.

"I can't just leave you here," he says.

"You can."

"Reid isn't here. When I rang him he was at the bar, so you don't have to worry about seeing him," he says, getting out of the car and walking around to open my door for me.

"Promise?"

"I promise, babe, come on."

We walk up the stairs and to the front of apartment number twenty eight. Ryan unlocks the door, and gently pushes me to enter before him. He turns on the lights and I walk in, checking the place out. It's spacious and beautifully decorated, sparsely but lovely just the same. The kitchen is black and white, with red bar stools.

"This is my room," he says opening the door to a large room, with a huge bed and probably the largest TV I've ever seen. He turns the TV on and tells me to sit, leaving the room, and returning minutes later with a vodka orange for me.

"Thanks," I say, taking a sip. I cringe when I realise it's mainly vodka. "If this is how you pour your drinks at the bar no wonder so many women want to go home with you," I joke. Ryan messes my hair up with his hand and then leaves to the bathroom. I finish my drink slowly, smiling when I hear Ryan out in the kitchen. I stand up, and wobble slightly, before walking out to the kitchen to ask for a refill.

"Ryan, I..." I trail off when I see Reid standing there. What the hell is he doing here? Yes, I know this is his apartment, but come on.

"What are you doing here?" he demands, eyeing my bare feet and my empty glass. I took my shoes off and left them in Ryan's room. When Ryan walks out a few seconds later, shirtless, I'll admit it doesn't look good. But when a girl walks up and stands next to Reid, I could care less how it looks.

I give Ryan the dirtiest look I can muster, but he just shrugs. "Reid, I thought you were at the bar."

Well, at least Ryan didn't lie to me.

"I'm sorry, I didn't know I was going to be interrupting something," he says in a cold tone. He looks gorgeous as always, wearing faded jeans and a black shirt. His hair is dishevelled, like someone was running their hands through it...

"Ryan, get dressed, and let's get out of here," I say, putting my hands on his back to push him towards his room door. I grab the bottle of vodka from the table, realising there's no way I'm standing here with Reid and his piece of ass, so I follow Ryan into his room.

"You going to watch?" he teases, pulling a fresh shirt out of his cupboard and shoving it on.

"Turnabout is fair play," I joke, not wanting to think about Reid.

Reid and another woman.

How stupid am I?

"Hey, you alright?" Ryan asks softly, doing up the buttons on his shirt.

I swallow hard before answering. "I'm fine." I take a sip of vodka straight from the bottle.

"Does this shirt look okay?" Ryan asks me. I can't help it, I start laughing.

The door suddenly bursts open, the sound making me jump.

"What are you doing here, Summer?" Reid asks, his teeth clenching with the effort.

I look at him but don't reply, taking another swig of vodka instead.

Who knew I was so classy? Apparently Reid brings out the best in me.

"I'm taking her out, Reid, she deserves a night out," Ryan says as he puts on his shoes.

Reid paces up and down, looking agitated. "Let it go, Reid. You need to let it go," Ryan says softly, a flash of sadness and regret crossing his expression.

"I can't," Reid states flatly.

"Reid?" I look up at the door to see *her* walk in. The blonde from the bar. I didn't even glance her way when I saw her in the kitchen, so I didn't recognize her, but it's definitely her. Shortish blonde hair, big brown eyes, a lot of makeup.

I hate her.

"Ryan," I say, my tone impatient.

"I'm done," he says, pushing his wallet into his snug fitting jeans.

"I'm surprised you can even fit that in there," I tell him, pursing my lips. I look anywhere but at Reid, because if I look at him, I'm going to lose it.

Ryan grins, turning around and doing a little ass shake. I force a giggle and then head towards the door, side stepping both Reid and his mysterious blonde. When I walk past, Reid gently takes hold of my arm. "Beauty," he says softly, his voice pleading.

Pleading for what?

"Let's go, Ryan," I say, walking to the front door, not looking behind me.

CHAPTER EIGHT

Could today get any more awkward? I'm sitting at my dad's dinner table, eating with him and his girlfriend. I feel like I'm a kid again, pissed at not having his attention.

"How's everything, Summer?" dad asks, seemingly interested.

"Fine." I take a sip of my soda.

"Do you need any money?" he asks kindly.

"No, thank you." I pull out my phone and see a text message from an unknown number.

"Okay, I know you're stubborn, but you know anything I have is yours," he says, his gaze never leaving me.

"Except your time, of course," I say without thinking. Jack looks surprised, and it annoys me further.

"I didn't think you wanted to spend any time with me. I had to pretty much beg you just to get you here for dinner," he says, the sadness in his tone making me feel guilty. My dad is pretty scary looking. Tall, built, bearded and tattooed. But he's a real softy, especially with me. He's never yelled at me or anything like that, although from what I've been told, it's only me he treats like that. I think it's from the guilt of never being there for me.

"Yeah, and when I do show up you don't even want one on one time with me, instead you have your girl here who I don't even like," I say in all honesty. I emphasise the girl part. When my dad looks shocked, I sigh dramatically.

How can he be so obtuse?

"Tina, leave me alone with my daughter," he says, his tone picking up strength when he addresses her.

"You can't be serious," she whines, glaring at me.

"Now," he says calmly, and she stands up to leave, making a big show of it. When she finally goes into the bedroom, slamming the door behind her, he looks straight at me, his gaze softening.

I feel like he is looking right through me right now.

"I knew you weren't fond of her, I thought it was just because of her age," he says.

"She's a bitch. She thinks I'm going to come between the two of you," I tell him.

"She said that?" he growls, starting to look angry. I shrug, not wanting to get into it.

"That's cos she knows nothing is more important to me than you and Xander. I know I haven't always been there for you, but not because I didn't want to be. Your mother told me I could only see you once a year, Summer. And I wasn't exactly in the position to ask for full custody. I didn't want to take you away from her anyway. I didn't want to pull you from the life you knew. I wanted you with me, trust me, but I didn't want to be selfish. After all was said and done, she was a good mother to you, so I took what I could. God, I used to wait until your birthday so I could see you. See how much you'd grown, how beautiful you were getting," he says, his voice wistful.

"Really?" I whisper, my voice breaking.

"Of course, Summer, you were my little girl. You *are* my little girl. There's nothing I won't do for you."

"She said you didn't care about me, you just left me to be with your new family," I say softly, my voice wavering. He slams his fist down on the table, making me jump.

"She lied, Summer," he growls, his face contorting in anger.

I exhale deeply, leaning my chin on my palm. "You cheated on her."

Jack noticeably flinches. "I did. My relationship with her wasn't working, but it had nothing to do with you. You were the only reason I stayed with her. You were my little princess, Summer, and she used you as a weapon against me."

"She told me the best thing a father can do for his daughter was love her mother," I say, my tone now emotionless. When I see a tear drop down my father's cheek, my own tears flow.

"I messed up, but I never stopped loving you, Summer." I get up from my chair and walk over to him, throwing my arms around him and burying my face in his neck. I cry as he keeps apologizing over and over again, making me cry further.

"I hate seeing you cry," he says gruffly, wiping my tears with his thumb.

"I'm sorry."

84

"Don't be sorry, baby girl. I want you in my life, I want to show you how much I love you. You make an old man proud."

"I want that, too," I admit. "And you're not that old."

He kisses me on my cheek.

"I've missed out on so much. Your mother sent me pictures and kept me updated, but I missed out on being there for you. I regret that we can't get that time back, but we have now. You've made me so happy by coming here, Summer."

When the sobs subside, my father and I talk, for what feels like the first time. We listen to each other, and we get to know each other.

And it's perfect.

"Xander tells me you have eyes for Reid." He doesn't look too happy about it.

"I had eyes for Reid." My heart hurts at the mere mention of him.

"He's a complicated kid, but a good one," my dad says, watching me carefully.

"He doesn't want me," I say, feeling sorry for myself.

"You are the most beautiful girl in the world, of course he wants you," he says, sounding defensive on my behalf.

"You have to think that, I'm your only daughter," I say, my lip twitching.

"Doesn't mean it's not the truth. I've known Reid for years, you know that? I was friends with his parents, before..."

"Before his mother died?" I add when he doesn't continue.

"Right. He's got a good heart, he loves his brothers more than anything," he says.

"Brothers?"

"Yeah, he had another brother. Younger. Reece. He passed away two years back," he says sadly.

"What?" I whisper. Reid lost his mother, and his baby brother? And his dad's in jail?

Shit. That's a lot of heart ache right there.

I scrub my face with my hand.

"You care about him a lot, don't you?" my dad asks, running his fingers through his beard.

"It doesn't matter."

"It does," he huffs.

"He needs to be willing to fight for me, dad, but he doesn't want to," I say, shrugging.

"I think he's doing enough fighting for other people, Sum, maybe he needs someone to fight for him," he says, a knowing look entering his eyes.

"You're supposed to be on my side," I complain, rolling my eyes.

"I'm always on your side, but if you had to pick a man, you could do a lot worse than Reid Knox."

"Is that so?" I mutter.

"Don't get me wrong, he hurts you, and he's dead," he says, an evil glint entering his eyes.

I sigh. "I don't know what's going to happen with us, to be honest."

"So, you don't like Tina, huh?" he asks, changing the subject.

I shake my head.

I never see Tina again.

CHAPTER NINE

I try to school my features, contain my surprise when I see Reid at the bar when I walk in. Guess he couldn't avoid me anymore. I nod my head at him in welcome, and put my bag in the office. When I don't see Ryan or Tag, I groan out loud. Looks like it's just Reid and me tonight. Well, hell. It's been a week since I saw Reid at his apartment, but he hasn't been far from my mind. When I got asked out on a date last night at work, I actually said yes. I need to move on, and I miss having Reid around.

"How have you been?" I ask him, noticing the dark circles under his eyes. He looks tired.

"Okay, you?" he asks me, throwing down the tea towel he was wiping the glasses with.

"I'm okay, I miss you, though," I blurt out, needing to be honest with him.

His face softens. "God, I miss you, too," he says quietly. So quietly I almost didn't hear it.

"Can we just be friends? Stop avoiding each other?" I ask him, putting myself out on a limb.

"Friends?" he repeats, a strange look flashing in his eyes.

"Sure, I mean. It has to be better than this, right?" I gesture with my hand between us. I hate the constant avoiding of each other and the awkwardness and him feeling so distant.

He nods once, but doesn't look too happy about it. "Where's Ryan?" I ask. Ryan has become one of my best friends. He looks out for me, and we always have fun together.

"He's out with his new girl of the week," Reid answers, watching my face carefully. I know what he's looking for, any signs of jealousy. He isn't going to find any though, cos Ryan and I are friends and nothing more.

"She's a babe," I say with a smirk, thinking back on last night when I met her for the first time. The chick was a knock out. I ended up high-fiving Ryan in congratulations, because he did well for himself.

"Are we okay?" Reid asks suddenly, his mood shifting.

"Sure," I say, the side of my lip quirking. What else can I say?

"I haven't seen you at the gym," he says. God, his eyes are so blue. Are they bluer than Ryan's? They seem so.

"I went once more with Xander but that's about it. I think I'm going to stick to doing Zumba at home." I start stacking glasses.

"I'm going to pretend I know what that is," he says.

"It's like a dance workout thing."

His eyebrows rise. "Sounds hot."

I smile, my eyes scanning the empty bar. "Never seen the place so dead."

"It gets like this now and again." He lifts his shoulder in a shrug.

"What do you want me to do?" I ask. The place looks clean enough to me.

"You can wipe down a few of the tables," he says. I nod, getting out the spray and towels and wiping down all the tables thoroughly. I pull out the vacuum and get to work, making sure the floor is spotless, too. When I can't find anything else to do, I go and stand next to Reid, who is going through receipts at the cash register. He looks up at me, his expression unguarded.

"I know I'm an asshole, Sum. God, you are so beautiful. I just, I need some time. Can you give me that?" he asks, his eyes so intense.

"I don't get what you want from me, Reid," I reply, not looking away.

"I want you, but I can't have you," he says, his expression now veiled.

"You can have me, I'm right here! You're the one pulling away, playing hot and cold with me." I really want to understand, but he's not giving me much.

"It's not the right time, I can't get involved with anyone right now." He slams the cash register shut.

"Exactly, so we can be friends. You can fuck whoever you want, and I can do the same," I say, gauging his reaction.

He doesn't look pleased. "Are you trying to tell me you're fucking someone?" he growls, and I see a flash of pain and regret before he masks his expression.

"What I'm saying is that it isn't any of your business," I say, my gentle tone softening the blow of my harsh words.

"Who?" he grates out, his jaw clenched.

"No one!" I huff, sighing in relief when a customer walks in. However, when I see its Reid's blonde my temper gets the best of me.

"Who is this bitch?" I ask Reid, saying it loud enough for her to hear.

"Don't talk to her like that, Summer," he snaps, walking over to the girl and talking to her in hushed tones.

What the hell?

I walk into the office and start sorting through papers, not wanting to see Reid act tender towards another woman. Why is she always around?

It takes about half an hour until Reid approaches me. "Summer, we've got customers."

Without saying a word, I put the papers down and head out the front, serving a couple of girls who had just turned legal.

"What can I get you?" I ask a cute dark haired guy. He looks to be about my age, with a lanky frame and bright blue eyes.

"I'll have a beer," he says, grinning.

"What kind?"

"How about you pick one for me," he says, leaning against the bar. I pick out the girliest beer I can find, and hand it to him. He chuckles, shaking his head at me, handing over the money.

"What's your name?" he asks.

"Summer, you?"

"Harlen, nice to meet you." He eyes me, taking a small sip of beer.

"You, too."

"I haven't seen you here before," he says.

"I'm kind of a new recruit," I tell him, pushing my hair behind my ear.

"Can I take you out?" he blurts out, flushing. I find myself leaning forward a little, endeared by his shy expression.

"No chance in hell, Harlen," comes a growl from behind me. I exhale deeply, causing my hair to blow in the air.

Harlen looks surprised. "She yours?"

"Are you questioning me?" Reid asks, steel in his tone.

Harlen shakes his head. "See you on Thursday, Reid," he says, throwing a longing glance my way before walking to a table with a few other guys.

I sigh. "That was really rude."

"You want a boy or a man, beauty?" he asks, his lips pursing.

"I just want you, Reid, but I don't always get what I want, do I? I learnt that at a young age. You need to stop with the whole 'if you can't have me, neither can anyone else' thing because it's selfish and I'm getting sick of it."

Reid scrubs his hand down his face, staying silent for a second before he replies. "You want me to say it's okay for you to be with another guy? Cos that's never going to happen. Ever."

I stomp my foot in frustration. "Where did your girlfriend go?" I sneer.

"She's not my girlfriend, Summer," he says patiently.

"Then who is she?" I demand.

"Why, you jealous?" he says, crossing his arms over his chest.

"What do you think?" I snap, copying his stance.

"She's not my girl, I haven't had a girlfriend since..." he trails off, looking put out that he let that slip.

"Since who?" I ask, dying with curiosity.

"No one," he says, avoiding eye contact.

"When?"

"About two years ago," he says. Two years ago? When he lost his brother?

"Okay," I say, stopping with the twenty questions.

"Okay?" he echoes, looking suspicious.

"Sure. Hey, tomorrow, can I come in to work a little late? I have a hair appointment."

"No problem. What you doing to it?" he asks, sounding like he genuinely wants to know.

"Cutting it."

He freezes, turning to stare at me. "How short?"

I show him with my hands. "Just above my shoulders."

"You're not cutting it," he says, frowning.

"I'm sorry?" I say slowly, sure I didn't hear him right.

"I love your hair, please don't cut it," he begs, taking a lock of my hair and staring at it.

I laugh at his forlorn expression. "So what? If I cut it you aren't going to find me attractive anymore?"

"Like that would ever happen," he mutters, running a finger down my cheek. "You don't know just how beautiful you are, Summer. Why do you think I call you beauty? You are something else, something special. A fucking treasure."

I get goose bumps from his words.

"Listen, I…"

I stop talking when I see a group of people walk in, the moment ruined.

*****

"I don't like it," Xander says for the tenth time.

"Can you act your age? And not like my father?" I scowl, pulling up the sweetheart neckline of my black dress. I run my fingers through my freshly trimmed hair, loving the softness and the texture of the layers.

"I'm your brother, it's my job to look after you. What if this asshole tries something?" he demands, looking like he's about to lose his cool.

"It's just a date! I'll be back in a couple of hours. I'm not going to bone him on the first date, Xander!" I explain, rolling my eyes.

Xander laughs, breaking the tension. "Keep your phone on you. Is it charged?"

"Yes, I will, and yes, it is. Calm down, baby brother," I say, leaning up on my tip toes and kissing him on the cheek.

"I'm never having daughters," he sulks, pouring himself a scotch.

I shake my head. "You're an old soul, Xander. Must have been that time you did in jail," I joke.

"Oh, come on. It was just one night," he says, his lip twitching.

"Well, you sure know how to make a first impression," I say dryly, causing his body to shake with laughter.

"Reid's not going to like this," he states when his laughter subsides.

"Not his business," I say, my voice wavering a little.

"There's things about Reid you don't know, I don't think you should give up on him," he says in a gentle tone.

"I thought you weren't a fan of Reid and me?"

"I wasn't. But he's different around you. And he's a scary mofo, he'll always protect you. I need my sister safe," he says.

The doorbell rings, and Xander rushes to answer it. Everyone is hinting about Reid, but no one will give me answers. It's driving me bat shit crazy. When I see it's my dad at the door and not my date, Lyle, I frown.

"Good, I caught you before your date arrives," my dad says, smiling evilly.

"This isn't prom, you guys," I say, rubbing my temples. I swear I feel a headache coming on.

"Yeah, but this is our first time sending you off with another man," Xander scoffs.

"You look beautiful, Summer Ray," Jack says, smiling happily.

"Please don't use my middle name again," I beg, causing both of them to laugh. "I'm serious. Summer Ray, come on," I groan.

"It suits you."

"Yeah, if I was a hippie." I slip my feet into my hot pink stilettos and put on a black cardigan.

"You ready to go, Xander?" dad asks him.

"Where are you two going?"

"We have some business on tonight," my dad answers. I walk into my bedroom to get my bag. When I walk back out I can hear them both whispering. I lean against the door straining to hear.

"Reid doesn't know about her going on a date, right?" Jack asks Xander.

"Nope."

"Good, he needs to be on his game tonight," dad says, sounding worried.

"He'll probably come here tonight, though. He did last time," Xander adds. I walk out, narrowing my eyes at the two of them.

"What's going on tonight?" I demand. The doorbell rings, and they both look relieved. When they both head to try and answer the door, I grab onto their shirts.

"No way. Goodnight, both of you. You have some explaining to do when I get back." I kiss them both on the cheek and then open the door. Lyle stands there, in dark denim jeans and a tight white top. I guess I'm a little overdressed.

"Hey, Lyle," I say smiling. He returns my smile, but then it suddenly drops. I glance behind me to see dad standing there, an intimidating aura surrounding him.

"I'm Jack Kane, you heard of me, boy?" he asks Lyle. Lyle swallows and nods twice. "Right. Take care of my girl."

"Yes, sir," Lyle says, swallowing so hard I can actually see the bob of his Adam's apple.

"Good," dad says, the tension clearing. We walk to Lyle's car, and I frown when he doesn't even bother to open the door for me.

"Where are we going?" I ask him once we both get in.

"I was going to take you out to dinner. But I got an invite for an event, so you're coming with," he says, glancing over at me like I should be happy.

"Okay."

"After meeting your father, I know you're going to like it. Fuck, I can't believe I'm rocking up with Jack Kane's daughter," he says, sounding almost giddy.

"What do you mean?" I ask.

"What? Oh, nothing."

"Explain," I demand.

"It's a surprise," he says, turning up the music so I can't talk.

Douchelord.

We stop at one of Lyle's friends' houses, where he makes me sit in the car for fifteen minutes. This is the worst date ever. I didn't even have dinner. Lyle finally returns and we drive to a dodgy looking warehouse.

"What is this place?" I ask, my eyes darting around. We walk inside and I see a large crowd of people. Lyle hands the door guy two tickets, and my skin crawls when he puts his arm around me.

"Tickets are normally two hundred dollars each," he brags.

"Good for you," I mutter under my breath. Lyle leads me to a different section, and when I look up I freeze.

There's a caged octagon, similar to the one we have at dad's gym, and right in the middle is Reid.

"Reid?" I whisper, my lips forming the word but no sound coming out. I watch as he faces off with another guy, who seems to be a tiny bit bigger than him.

"What is this?" I ask Lyle, who flashes me a confused expression. The fight begins and I close my eyes, leaning back onto a wall. I hear cheering, and yelling, so I take a peak, just in time to see Reid punch his opponent right in the face. I grin, but it only lasts a few seconds, because then Reid takes a hit to his stomach.

I close my eyes shut again.

I can't watch this. Can I?

When I open my eyes, Lyle is lost, swept away with the crowd. He just left me. Fucking asshole.

I watch as they circle each other, bouncing on their heels. Reid suddenly lifts his leg in a kick, pulls back, then comes at full force with another punch. He gets his opponent up against the cage with his arms around him, punching at the back of his head. The crowd goes wild, and I turn my head to look for Lyle once more, but can't see him anywhere. I glance back towards the cage, where Reid is the victor. He has blood dripping from his nose, but besides that, he looks untouched. The other guy, however, looks completely battered.

Why does Reid do this?

And why keep it a secret? Is this why he won't be with me?

A growl escapes my mouth when I see no other than Xander, Ryan, Dash and my dad standing around Reid.

I see red. I don't think I've ever been so mad and hurt in my entire life. And when the blonde chick steps up next to Reid, I lose it.

It takes me a good ten minutes to walk over to them, the crowd bumping me and I can't walk as fast as I wish in these four inch heels. I'm tempted to take them off, but looking at the floor I would probably need a tetanus shot. When I finally near them, Reid's gone missing. Cursing under my breath, I walk up to the group of men that have become my life.

"Fancy meeting you all here," I say dryly, containing my emotions.

Four pairs of eyes glance at me, with emotions ranging from shock to guilt.

"What are you doing here?" My father growls, looking angry. *He's* angry?

"This is where my date brought me," I say, sneering the word date.

"What the fuck?" Xander roars, looking me over.

"I'm fine," I assure him, throwing accusing glances at each of them. My dad and Xander look angry, Ryan looks apologetic and Dash is smiling at me, looking like he's relieved I finally know.

"Where is he?" I ask, not needing to explain who I'm talking about. When they don't answer, I raise my voice. "Where the fuck is he?"

"Come on, I'll take you," Ryan says, walking over to me. He tries to take my arm but I pull away.

"Don't be like that, babe," he says sadly, his brow furrowing.

"You guys all lied to me. What, you don't trust me?"

"Of course we trust you, this isn't exactly the place for a woman," he says in a gentle tone that grates on my nerves.

"I'm not fragile, Ryan." He opens the exit for me and I walk out.

I see Reid leaning against the wall, wiping blood from his nose. He throws the towel over his shoulder, and then the blonde leans up and kisses him on his mouth.

I turn away, as fast as I can, tears forming in my eyes. Ryan mutters a curse behind me, and then I hear him yelling Reid's name. I let myself fall into the crowd, until I find the entrance we came in from. I run out, into the car park, and look around, wondering what the hell I'm supposed to do now. My phone keeps ringing and I see Reid, Ryan, Xander, Dash and my dad's numbers pop up. When I see Lyle leaning against his car, I grin. What an unlikely saviour.

"Lyle, I need a ride somewhere and you aren't getting any action tonight," I notify him when I approach his car.

He scowls. "Fine. Only cos your dad will probably kill me otherwise." I get into his car, exhaling in relief when we get onto the main road. I put my phone on silent, not wanting to talk to anyone right now.

"Why did you bring me there?" I ask him.

"I always come to the fights when I can, and I didn't wanna miss it over a date. Then when I found out who your dad was I figured you'd wanna go anyway," he explains.

"Why? What does it have to do with my dad?"

"Your dad runs the fights, Summer," he says, looking at me like I'm insane. I take a minute to absorb this information. Dad organizes these fights.

Well, that's fucking news to me.

"Where are we going?" he asks, his eyes on the road.

"I don't wanna go home," I sulk.

"You can come crash at my dorm room," he offers.

I must look suspicious because he laughs at my expression. "My roommate is away, you can sleep in his bed."

"You sure?"

He nods, his eyes darting to me, then back on the road. "Don't worry, I won't let anything happen to you. I actually like my balls."

"Where was that line of thought when you left me alone in the middle of the chaos?"

"I lost you, I tried to find you. I texted you, too," he says.

I check my phone and there's indeed a message from him asking where I am. I ignore the twenty six missed calls and check my messages. Five from Reid, which I don't bother to read. Instead I text Xander and tell him I'm safe, and I'll be home tomorrow. He replies instantly, saying to call him and he'll come and get me, but I ignore it.

"So they fight for money?" I assume.

"Yep. Entrance is two hundred each, and that goes into the prize money for the winners," he explains.

"What do you know about Reid Knox?" I ask.

"Besides that I wouldn't wanna mess with him?"

I roll my eyes. "He wins a lot?"

"Undefeated," he answers, and I'm not surprised one bit.

"Anything else you can tell me?"

"That's pretty much all there is to it. They follow MMA rules, they fight, and someone wins. That about sums it up." He parks the car and we walk to his dorm room. I'm surprised to find it fairly tidy.

"I'll order us some pizza, you can relax," he says, pushing me gently towards the couch.

Turns out Lyle isn't so bad after all.

CHAPTER

TEN

I wave bye to Lyle, after thanking him for letting me crash the night before. Shoes in hand, I walk barefoot to the front door, digging in my clutch for the house key. Before I can find it, the door opens and a furious looking Reid stands there, watching Lyle's car drive off. I feel a twinge of guilt when I take in his appearance. Dark shadows under his eyes, his face slightly pale, and his hair sticking up at all angles, he looks like he could use a good night's rest. His nose is also red and swollen, where he must have been hit last night at the fight. He's shirtless, and barefoot. I walk past him, gritting my teeth when he doesn't move aside, so I have to slide my body against his. He grabs a tight hold on my wrist before I can move out of reach.

"Where were you?" he asks hoarsely, his eyes full of pain.

"Out."

He curses and lets go of me, but follows me to my room.

"Where is everyone?" I ask, placing my bag on my bed.

"Bed, they only went to sleep an hour ago. We were all worried, Summer."

"I texted Xander and told him I was fine," I say, lifting my shoulder in a slight shrug.

"How easy would it have been for someone else to send that message from your phone?" he growls, threading his fingers together behind his neck.

"Why would someone do that?" I ask, surprised at his paranoia.

"I have enemies, Summer," he says, his tone laced with anger.

He's angry at me? Oh, this is rich. I shake my head at him, not quite believing this turn of events.

"Why are you here?" I ask, proud of myself for keeping my voice steady.

"About last night, it wasn't what it looked like." He reaches with his hand to touch me. I take a step back, hating the defeated look that comes over him.

"That's a new line," I say, the sarcasm in my tone evident.

"She kissed me. I pushed her away..." he says, looking tortured.

"Okay?" I gesture for him to continue talking.

"And you were on a fucking date, so I didn't even do anything wrong," he bites out.

"So you lied to me, a million times over, then you get caught kissing another girl, but you didn't do anything wrong. I'm so happy we aren't actually together!" I spit out. My lip trembles, giving away just how hurt I am.

"You don't mean that," he says softly, his face drawn.

"You don't know me."

"I know you," he replies softly, studying me.

"So, you're an underground fighter," I say, changing the subject.

He curses, watching my face intently.

"How does that work exactly?" I ask, wanting to hear it from him.

"We meet up at different locations. Spectators pay entry, two hundred dollars each, and then that money is used as the prize money. It's just something I've been doing for a while," he says with a slight shrug, trying to play it off as no big deal.

I blink twice, pondering his words. "Why all the secrecy?"

"There's more to it, beauty, but that's all you need to know, alright? Now come here," he says as he hops onto my bed, pulling the sheet up for me to climb in.

"Why are you always with her?" I ask him in a small voice.

"I don't like her like that, trust me," is all he says.

"Fine, but she obviously likes you like that," I snap.

"I set her straight, she won't be trying that shit again, okay?" he says in a soothing tone.

I sit down on the bed next to him. "You hurt me. You kissed her. Her fucking lips were on yours."

"I fucked up. I'm going to fuck up. But I wanna try," he whispers, pulling me down so my head is on his chest.

"You wanna try what?" I ask, my voice soft and unsure.

"I wanna try with you, I don't want you on dates with anyone else. You're mine, beauty." He tightens his hold on me.

"I can't," I say in a timid voice.

"We'll talk after a few hours' sleep, I was up all night," he says. I lie back on the bed, staring at the ceiling. When he pulls me into his arms I hold my breath, wanting to relax into him but knowing that I shouldn't. I can't let my guard down around this man. He has the power to break me, if I give it to him. I'm already in over my head.

That's my last thought before I fall asleep.

*****

I wake up two hours later, slowly extracting myself from Reid's arms. Xander is standing in the kitchen with our dad, both of them draining a cup of coffee.

"Mornin'," I say, heading to the fridge and pulling out an apple juice box.

"What happened last night will not happen again, Summer," my dad grinds, staring at me with an intense expression.

"What, you mean every single person I know in this town lying to me?"

"Sum…" Xander says, his forehead crinkling.

"Why was it some big secret? So you run some illegal underground fight club, who cares? I thought you guys were up to much worse from the stories mum told me," I say dryly. I open my juice box and take a sip. Both Kane men stay silent for a few moments, and the only sound that can be heard in the kitchen is me drinking from my straw.

"What did she say about me?" my dad finally rumbles.

"That you were a biker, a drug dealer, a criminal, a cheater, a womanizer... I could go on," I tell him. And I could. Those were probably the nicer things she said about him, and we all know the cheating part is true.

My dad slams down his coffee mug and walks to the front door, looking pissed off. He pulls out a cigarette on the way.

"Reid didn't want me saying anything, sis, and neither did Jack," Xander says, coming towards me. He wraps me in his arms and kisses me on the head. "In the beginning Reid was all for telling you everything, but when you two got involved, he decided he didn't want you to see him like that. Sometimes the other fighters play dirty, I wouldn't be surprised if they tried something if they saw you hanging about, so it was for your safety, as well."

"Well, you made me look stupid. I had to find out from Lyle. And I don't like being lied too. If it's not safe for me, how come that blonde chick gets to go?" I ask, staring up at him.

"She's involved," he says, kissing me on the head again.

"How?" I demand.

"You should ask Reid, these aren't really my secrets to tell. Or ask Ryan," he says. Ryan. Another person on my shit list.

"Reid was really worried about you last night, Summer. You were selfish, next time answer your phone, okay?" he says, his voice carrying a tone he's never spoken to me in before. He leaves the kitchen and walks down the hall.

"Maybe if Reid kept his mouth to himself," I mutter to myself under my breath. When dad doesn't return after thirty minutes I walk outside to find him standing there, staring at his motorcycle.

"I'm sorry, dad." I don't want him to be mad at me. He raises his head and I don't like the blank look on his expression.

"I'm not perfect, Summer."

"I don't expect you to be," I say, and it's true, I don't. I walk over to him, and lean my head against his chest.

"I'm happy I came here, dad. And you don't have to walk on eggshells around me anymore, just be yourself. I won't judge anymore, okay?" I say into his chest.

"I want you to be comfortable here, not have to worry about our bullshit," he replies, leading me back into the house.

"Well, I'm in it, so you're going to have to get used to it. You're not getting rid of me," I say with a cheeky smirk.

"Good, cos I've never been happier Summer. Finally have my family together," he rumbles, clearing his throat. I don't think my dad is generally an emotional guy, and I smile knowing he only gets like this around me. To him, I will always be his little girl, the one he didn't get to have in his life on a permanent basis.

"Where's Reid?" he asks, about to head home.

"Asleep."

He sighs. "Alright, I hope you know what you're doing."

I have no idea what I'm doing.

I say bye to dad and then walk back into the bedroom, where Reid is still fast asleep on his stomach. His face looks so relaxed as he sleeps, even with the slight bruising on his face. The sheet is sitting just over his ass, so I get a clear view of his toned back.

I've never seen a more perfect man.

I go through my phone, seeing a message from Ryan saying to call him when I wake up. I delete the rest of the messages from last night, and clear all my call lists. I have this thing about erasing everything, I hate having a heap of old messages sitting in my inbox.

"Mornin', beauty," Reid says, his voice thick with sleep.

"Morning. How's your face?" I ask, frowning.

"Its fine." He sits up in the bed. "Come here."

I walk over to the bed and sit next to him, his hands grabbing me before my butt hits the mattress.

"Come spend the day with me at my place," he whispers into my ear.

"What exactly changed between yesterday and today, Reid?" I ask, completely confused with the situation.

"I'm done fighting myself. I want you so bad, Summer. You're mine, I've known it since the moment I laid my eyes on you."

"You were a jerk to me that day," I remind him.

"I didn't want to want you," he says, and even though he's being honest, it kinda hurts.

"That's romantic," I say dryly.

"It's real, Summer," he replies, kissing me on the cheek. The light stubble on his face tickles my face.

"I need to know about her first," I demand, and something instantly shifts in the air.

"She's my brother's ex-girlfriend," he admits after a few moments of silence. Ryan's ex? Why didn't he say anything?

"What's her name?" I ask.

"Jade."

"Why is she always around you? And why did you let her kiss you?" I ask, my voice gaining steel.

"I pushed her away, Summer," he growls, and I can tell he's getting annoyed. Well, too damn bad.

"Clearly not soon enough!" I snap.

"Who did you go on a date with last night?" he counters, turning it around on me.

"What's your problem? We aren't even together," I say defensively, narrowing my eyes at him.

"Exactly," he smirks, obviously feeling like he won this round.

"That doesn't mean it didn't hurt, Reid," I say softly, avoiding looking at him.

He curses. "I didn't want her. I only want you, Summer. You've gotten under my skin."

"At least I didn't kiss my date," I say with a scowl.

"And you won't get a chance to," he says with finality. I want to stay mad, but we stare at each other for a few moments, and as usual his eyes penetrate through my every defence.

What is it about him?

"Will you come to my next fight?" he asks, suddenly looking a little unsure. His fingers drum on my comforter, waiting for me to reply.

"I have to warn you, I closed my eyes through most of the one last night," I admit, scrunching my nose. Reid chuckles, shaking his head at me in amusement.

"How often do you fight?" I ask.

"There's a fight on every week, but I usually go once a fortnight or sometimes once a month. There are only certain opponents I'm interested in fighting," he tells me, tracing down my collarbone with his finger. When his finger reaches the top of my breast, I raise an eyebrow.

"Where does that finger think it's going?" I ask, smiling.

"I want you, when you're ready," he says, kissing me on my temple.

"And if I'm ready right now?"

"I'll know when you're ready, beauty. Now get ready, cos I'm taking you to my house." He gets out of the bed and walks out of my room.

CHAPTER ELEVEN

"Can you at least look at me?" Ryan asks, standing next to me as I take a handful of popcorn.

I glance up at him, sighing like it's a big deal. "What, Ryan?"

"Don't be mad, babe, come on. I had to follow my brother's wishes and he didn't want me telling you anything," he says, his eyes pleading with mine, begging for me to understand.

"You all made me look stupid," I grumble, sliding over on the couch so he can take a seat next to me.

"That wasn't our intention," he says, grabbing a handful of popcorn.

"So I've heard."

"Don't be stubborn and just forgive me," he says, throwing me one of his panty dropping smiles.

"Doesn't work on me, Ryan, but nice try."

He laughs, and then sobers. "I'll make it up to you, alright, babe?"

"You better."

Reid walks out, freshly showered, in a pair of basketball shorts slung low on his lean hips. I sigh in appreciation.

"Why don't you drool over me like that?" Ryan mock sulks.

"You just don't do it for me, Ry," I tease.

"I look exactly like him!" He chuckles, shoving another hand of popcorn in his mouth.

"No, you don't, I think your beer drinking is causing your abs to disintegrate," I joke, laughing when I see the look on Ryan's face. He narrows his eyes at me, and runs his hand up his abs, lifting the shirt up with the movement.

"Don't think so babe, trust me, I've been getting no complaints," he says, wiggling his eyebrows suggestively.

"Don't you have somewhere to be, Ryan?" Reid asks expectantly.

"Nope. I'm good right here, with my two fave people," he says, smiling.

Reid grunts, and inserts himself next to me on the other side. "Hey, beauty," he says, his lip tilting upwards.

I get butterflies every time he calls me that.

"Hey," I say in a soft voice, his scent engulfing me. "You smell good," I blurt out.

Reid's eyes smile at me. "What are we watching?" he asks, putting his arm around me and pulling me closer towards him.

I press play on the remote. "The Notebook."

They both object.

"This is our punishment, isn't it?" Reid asks, heaving a heavy sigh.

113

I grin. Ryan mumbles something about me being evil, while Reid raises an eyebrow in amusement.

Then we watch the movie.

*****

Reid opens the door for me as we walk into the restaurant. This is our first official date, and I'm a little nervous. I play with the charm on my handbag, twisting it around my fingers. We sit in a booth, side by side.

"I'm pretty sure you're meant to sit opposite me," I say, grinning.

"Then I can't touch you, so it doesn't work for me."

"Who are you and what have you done with Reid?" I joke, nudging him with my elbow.

"It's me," he whispers into my ear, then proceeds to bury his face in the crook of my neck and shoulder. A shiver of pleasure takes over my body.

"Reid!" I chastise, looking around to see if anyone is watching.

"So innocent," he croons, looking pleased. I realize that this is Reid with his guard down. He's letting me see him, without all the shields he usually has in place. The thought makes me feel lucky, that he chose to share this side of himself with me.

"What are we eating?" I ask as I look over the menu. We both order our meals when the waitress arrives.

"Does it annoy you that I'm older than you?" he asks once our drinks arrive.

"Does it annoy you that I'm younger than you?" I return.

"No, nothing about you annoys me," he says, pausing. "No, that's a lie."

I slap his arm playfully. "It doesn't bother me. You're what, twenty three, right?"

"Yes. That's four years older than you," he says, rubbing his hands over his face.

"I know, I can do math. And it's not that bad," I say defensively, sipping at my apple juice.

"It doesn't matter anyway," he says, staring into my eyes.

"Why?"

"In too deep," is all he says.

Our food soon arrives and we dig in. I get a message from Ryan, who's mad he couldn't come with us, and is instead stuck at the bar. I start laughing when I see the picture of him making a sad face. Reid groans when I show him.

"I feel bad he's at the bar by himself," I say around a mouth of mash potato.

"We can stop by afterwards."

"Sounds good. Where's Tag tonight?" I ask.

"He has his kid for the night," Reid says, watching me as I lick my fork. My eyes dart to the middle of the room when I hear my name being called.

Lyle.

Oh, shit.

He walks over, smiling warmly, until he sees who my date is.

"I guess now I know why you were asking about him," he mutters, clearing his throat.

"Hey, Lyle," I say, not wanting to be rude. He did help me out the other night, and he ended up being pretty cool.

"Reid, this is Lyle," I introduce, sighing when I see the daggers Reid is shooting at Lyle.

Lyle shifts on his feet, looking nervous. "I, uh. I just wanted to say hello. I guess I'll see you around, Summer," he says, walking away as quickly as he can.

"That was rude," I say, the air in the room so thick and uncomfortable, it's making me feel awkward.

"That's who you went on a date with?" he asks incredulously.

"Yeah."

"He's a kid," Reid snaps.

"Actually, he's my age," I say, cringing.

Reid curses and stares down at his plate. His jaw tenses and he stays silent, ignoring me.

"Reid. The date didn't work out, so we ended up hanging out as friends," I say softly, trying to diffuse his anger.

"You stayed the night with him?" he asks, more like a statement then a question.

"Well, yeah, I slept in his roommate's *empty* bed," I say.

"Fucking hell," he growls, his grip on the table turning his knuckles white.

"Well, maybe if you weren't kissing Jade and keeping secrets from me, I would have never gone on a date with anyone!" I yell, losing my temper.

116

"You know, Summer, when you forgive someone, the decent thing to do is not throw it back in their face every fucking chance you get. You think I don't regret it? Don't feel like shit about keeping you in the dark? And having to see Jade kiss me, even though I pushed her off me?"

His words make me feel like complete shit.

"Reid…"

"Let's go," he says, standing up walking to the register to pay. He doesn't even look back, or wait for me. I grab my handbag and walk to the front, following him outside to his car. He opens the door for me, even in his anger, and I get in without a word.

"Can you take me home?" I ask, my voice uneven.

He drums his fingers on the steering wheel, but doesn't answer me. Then he exhales loudly. "I don't want you to go, yet."

"You have a funny way of showing it," I say, looking out the window to distract myself from his handsome profile.

"I just don't like the thought of you out with another guy, sleeping at his fucking house. I'm sorry," he says, his eyes on the road. I glance at him, the scar on his jaw clearly noticeable from this angle. I lean over and run my finger along it, hating that he flinches and moves his face away.

"It's clear by all your shit I put up with that I only want you, Reid, no need to be jealous," I say, rolling my eyes.

"I'm not jealous," he huffs.

"Of course you aren't, baby," I coo.

Reid grins. "That's the first time you've called me baby."

"You like it?"

He nods, the shift in his mood obvious. "Okay, maybe I was a little bit jealous," he admits.

"Trust me, I know," I say with a smirk. Reid suddenly pulls the car over.

"What are you doing?" I gape, my eyes going wide. He smiles at me before leaning over and tangling one hand in my hair. His other hand tilts my chin up, as he brings his lips to my own. He kisses me gently, three times, before going in deeper, opening my mouth and tasting. When he pulls his lips away I'm left breathless and wanting more.

"So beautiful," he murmurs, pulling back onto the road.

"What was that for?" I ask, touching my lips.

"I've always wanted to kiss that smirk off your face," he says, grinning.

"Well, you did just that." Now it's him looking smug.

He puts on some music, and a Nine Inch Nails song flares through the speakers.

"What music do you like?" he asks me.

"A bit of everything. But I mainly listen to rap music."

"Rap?" he repeats, cringing.

"Yes, rap," I say defensively. When he starts laughing I scowl.

"There is nothing wrong with rap music," I tell him.

He lifts a shoulder in a shrug. "Just didn't see you as a rap kinda girl."

"What kinda girl am I?"

"Mine," he says, smiling. I stare at his profile for a moment, a feeling of contentment taking over me. This moody, amazing, sexy, sweet man is all mine.

"Does that caveman shit work on other women?" I ask.

"I wouldn't know, you're the first one I've ever felt possessive of," he says.

"Hmm."

"What are you thinking about?" he asks, turning his head to me.

"You."

"What about me?" he asks.

"Are you ever going to tell me how you got the scar?" I decide to ask.

Reid is silent for a few minutes before answering. "I'll tell you when I'm ready, okay?"

"Okay." I smile when he takes my hand into one of his, threading our fingers together. I know this is him telling me, although he may need time, he isn't going to shut me out, and I appreciate it.

When we arrive at the bar, I find that it's actually pretty busy. Poor Ryan.

"Maybe you should hire someone else?" I tell Reid, eyeing all the cars parked out front.

"Yeah, I had a few people apply," he says, opening the door for me to enter.

"What about Xander or Dash?" I ask.

"Dash is a full time mechanic, I don't think he would wanna work at the bar. I can ask Xander," he says. We walk up to the bar, and I offer Ryan an apologetic smile. Reid was meant to work tonight, but insisted on taking me out to dinner, and Ryan said it was no problem. I tie my hair up in a ponytail, and wash my hands before starting to serve the few customers still waiting. Reid heads into the back, needing to stock up on a few things.

"How was dinner?" Ryan asks in between customers.

I make a vodka sunrise as I answer. "It was good!"

"Didn't even bring any back for me," he sulks.

"You guys should start serving food here. Like chips, battered prawns and club sandwiches," I tell him, hoping for this outcome on one or more occasions.

Ryan chuckles. "We should, shouldn't we? I'm sure if you ask Reid he might."

Speaking of the devil, Reid walks out of the office, holding a stack of bottles and putting them in the fridge. When he bends over I get a nice view of his ass, which I happily ogle. I sigh in admiration, until Ryan nudges me, and gestures to a waiting customer.

"What can I get you?" I ask the woman. She has red hair, and bright pink lipstick on, most of it smudged onto her chin. Classy.

"Nothing here I haven't had before, sweetheart," she purrs, her eyes on Reid's ass.

"I'm sure there's no one you haven't had, now get your eyes off my man's ass," I tell her calmly, facing her head on.

Her eyes widen in surprise, and then narrow. "Never knew he liked them so young."

"Yeah, I guess his taste has improved," I mutter. She laughs, more like a cackle, and I'm about to tell her to fly off on her broom when my brother walks in.

"Xander, what happened?" I ask, running over to him. He's definitely been in a fight. His knuckles are bloody and battered, and his lip is cut and swollen.

He shrugs, playing off my concern. "Don't worry about it, sis, just a small incident." Reid walks over and tells Xander to go into the office.

"Reid…"

"Stay here, beauty, let me talk to him," he says softly, looking concerned. Ryan gently takes my arm and leads me back behind the bar. I see him do a double take when he takes in the face of the girl I was about to serve before.

"What the fuck are you doing here?" he growls at her, his face contorting in anger.

She puts her hands up in submission. "I'm just here for a drink."

"You're never just here for a drink," Ryan says, calming down.

"You think he was going to take me back after what happened?" she asks dryly.

"No, I guess not," Ryan says, reluctance in his tone. He pours her a drink anyway, and doesn't say another word to her.

"I still care about him, Ryan," she says, her eyes softening. She wait for Ryan to respond, but after he gives her nothing, she turns her back on us and leaves.

"What was that about?" I ask him, pissed that I'm left in the dark *again*. When he doesn't reply I storm to the office. Just as I pull the door open, Xander walks out, bumping into me.

"You okay?" I ask gently, lifting my hand to touch his face.

"Fine, Sum," he says with a smile. I look behind him to Reid, who has a pensive look on his face.

"What happened?" I demand.

"Went to a girl's house, her ex came over and we got into it," my brother answers, casual as ever.

"Do we have a first aid kit here?"

"Sis, don't fuss over me. I'm going home, and I'm fine." He kisses me on top of my head. "Cute having you worrying about me, though."

"I'm always worried about you," I say gently, eyeing his busted lip.

I look at Reid and say, "I'm going to go home with Xander, okay?"

He frowns, but nods. I walk up to him and kiss him on the cheek. "See you tomorrow?"

"Yeah, I'll come over and bring you lunch."

"Sounds good."

Xander and I go straight home, where I take care of his face and knuckles, and tell him to go to bed. After grumbling and growling at me, he finally listens, and I smile as his bedroom door closes.

I love being a big sister.

CHAPTER TWELVE

After my first class, I sit in the library, going over everything I learnt today. My human biology is a little rusty, and I'm definitely going to be doing a lot of studying.

Someone takes a seat opposite me, which is a little weird considering there are multiple empty tables. I lift my gaze and see it's a guy who looks to be in his early twenties. He has dark hair and eyes, a strong jaw and high cheekbones. His arms are bulky with muscle, not my type, but I can still appreciate his looks. My lip curving into a slight smile, I turn back down to my books. When I feel his eyes on me, I look up to see him studying me.

"It's rude to stare," I whisper, raising an eyebrow.

He tilts his head at me, and I'm curious about the indecision I see flash over his expression. He looks down at his own book and opens it, not saying anything back to me, so I continue with my own work. After an hour, I stand up, flashing a smile before I leave. I get in my car and drive straight to the bar. I have an hour before I start my shift, so I have time to change and sneak in a few kisses with Reid.

Singing along to Paula Deanda's 'Easy', I park my car and hop out, surprised to see Xander standing out the front, watching me. Ever since the fight Xander has been keeping a closer eye on me, and I have no idea why. I walk up to him, grinning as I see him wearing the new T-shirt I bought him.

"You're wearing it!" I say in greeting.

"Told you I love it, and I meant it."

"Good. You're a bit early to start drinking, bro," I say, stepping up on my tip toes to kiss him on the cheek. I pull my satchel off my shoulder, holding it in my hands.

"Everyone is here," he says, following me inside. I walk in and beam, because he's right, everyone is here. My dad, Dash, Ryan, Reid and a few of their other friends. Tag is at the bar alone, currently texting on his phone as usual. I say hello to everyone, laughing when Ryan runs up to hug me first.

"What's the occasion?" I ask Reid as I walk up to him and give him a peck on the lips.

"Got an important fight this weekend, beauty," he says, watching my face for my reaction.

"Am I invited to this one?" I ask dryly, a little bite in my tone.

"I hope you'll come to every fight from now on," he says, gripping me by my hips and pulling me down onto his lap. "But you'll have to stay with the guys, not going anywhere alone, you hear me?"

"I'm sure I can manage that."

"You okay with this?" he asks softly, and I know he means the whole fighting thing.

"Does it matter?" I reply, knowing that it doesn't. This means something to Reid, and there's no way I'm going to stand in his way. My mother once told

125

me there's no point trying to change a man. Either take him as he is, or find someone who you wouldn't want to change. This is Reid, and I'll take him as he comes. As long as he doesn't cheat on me, or anything like that, and he treats me well and we make each other happy, I'll support him. Yes, I'm worried about him getting hurt, but it's his decision, not mine.

"You know it does," he says into my throat. I look up and catch my dad watching me, so I quickly push Reid away. Awkward.

"How was class, Summer?" dad asks, smiling at my obvious discomfort.

"It was good, I know I'm going to enjoy it," I tell him.

"Proud of you," he says, lifting up his drink in a toast.

Trying not to get emotional, I say thank you, and clear my throat. Reid squeezes my thigh, obviously seeing right through me. I can't help it though, I never thought I would see the day when I'd hear my dad say things like that to me. We shoot the shit for a little while, until it's time for me to start my shift. I change, clock in, and then take over from Tag, who heads out for his break.

The night passes quickly, and before I know it, it's closing time. Ryan is sitting at the bar, going over some paperwork, while Reid is doing stock take. Tag already left to pick his kid up. He showed me pictures of his daughter, and she is absolutely beautiful. Her birthday is coming up and I make a mental note to buy her a gift. I finish wiping down all the counters when I see Jade standing at the entrance, knocking on the locked door.

"Ryan, why is Jade at the door?" I ask him, raising an eyebrow. He walks around the bar, and towards the door, unlocking it and letting her enter.

"What are you doing here?" he asks her, his tone neither friendly nor hostile.

"I haven't seen you or Reid in a while so I thought I would drop by," she says, sounding a little unsure. I slap the cloth down on the table and walk to the back. Reid is sitting there, writing furiously in a notebook. He looks adorable, his brow furrowing in concentration.

"Jade is here," I announce, trying to keep a poker face.

"What?" he asks, standing up. I can tell by the look on his face he wasn't expecting her.

I walk back out without answering, just in time to hear her say, "It's not fair I don't get to be in Reid's life because of her insecurities!" Her pale face goes red, and it's not a very attractive look.

"That's enough," Reid growls, walking up behind me and putting his arms around me.

"Summer, this is Jade. Jade, Summer is my woman, my first priority. You need to understand that," he says, pulling me closer against his chest.

"So, what, you and I can't even be friends anymore?" She gasps, tears forming in her eyes. I look at Ryan, who looks agitated. I'm so confused right now, isn't she Ryan's ex?

"Jade, why are you being so fucking difficult?" Reid sighs, letting me go and lacing his hands behind his head.

"Because this bitch came along and stole my only connection to my dead boyfriend! We had a plan, Reid, and this is fucking it all up!" she screeches, and I cringe. Dead boyfriend? Fuck. Reid's brother that passed away, Reece. This is his ex-girlfriend?

"If you cared so much about your ex-boyfriend why were you trying to kiss his brother?" I spit out, feeling guilty when her face pales. She clutches her hands over her chest dramatically, and her bottom lip trembles.

"Summer," Reid admonishes, and then I really lose my temper.

"So don't Summer me! I assumed she was Ryan's ex, since you didn't specify which brother, and now she's playing the guilt card? Well, she didn't look fucking guilty when she was trying to kiss you! This act she's pulling!" I gesture to her. "It's not working. I hate manipulative bitches," I growl the last word, stepping away from Reid.

"You don't know anything, you have been in their lives for a second! I've been here for years," she says smugly, her damsel in distress routine ending.

"This isn't a competition," I say, my palms clenching into fists.

"Well if it is, you lose. They won't choose you over me!" she snaps, crossing her arms over her chest.

"Jade, that's enough!" Reid roars, clearly having had enough drama. I ignore him and walk over to Ryan, really needing to talk to him in that moment.

"Ryan, can you take me home?" I ask him. I see Ryan look over my head to Reid, before looking down at me, grimacing.

"I want to, babe, but I think my brother will kill me in my sleep," he mock whispers. I turn around and pin Reid with a stare that would cause a lesser man to tremble.

"Ryan is taking me to your place, you deal with this," I tell him, daring him to argue.

"Fine," he grits, "but you aren't going to use this against me later." I roll my eyes, unable to deny that the man knows me pretty damn well. He walks over to me and kisses me deeply, his hands tangling in my hair. I pull away.

"See you soon," I say, walking to the front door. Ryan catches up, and we walk together to his car. We don't say anything until we're both inside the car and he starts the engine.

"Begin your hundred questions," he grumbles, reversing the car.

"She was your brother's ex," I start.

"Yes."

"When he passed away..." I look at him as I say it, watching several emotions cross his face.

"I'm sorry," I say quietly.

"Go on."

"She still stayed friends with the both of you. What I want to know, is why she and Reid are more attached to each other, and you..."

"I've let go of the anger. That's the truth. When Reece died, we were both devastated. We felt anger, sorrow, pain, guilt. He was our baby brother, and we couldn't protect him. We wanted someone to pay for his death, someone to blame. Jade felt all of those things, too, and she and Reid now have a common

129

goal. I felt the same at the start, but after a year I realized Reece sure as hell wouldn't want this for us, our mother wouldn't want this, either. So I pulled out of the fighting ring, and I'm trying to move on with my life. I'll always love and remember Reece, but this obsessive need for revenge isn't what any of us need," he explains. I'm left confused.

"What does the fighting have to do with your brother and revenge?" I ask. Ryan gives me a sympathetic glance, realizing Reid has told me pretty much nothing.

"Reece was the one who participated in the underground fighting. Reid was studying business, and I was about to enrol in the police force. Reece had a fight one night, and he died in that ring," he says, his voice wavering on the last sentence.

"So Reid wants to, what? Fight because his brother did?"

"No, Reid wants to fight the current champion. Which happens to be the guy who killed Reece," he says bitterly.

My mouth opens wide in shock. "And Jade is egging him on?"

"Yes."

That little bitch.

"What if something happens to him?" I ask.

Ryan shrugs. "I've tried to talk him out of it, to let it go, but Reid does what Reid wants to do."

"More secrets," I say, unable to hide the bitterness in my voice.

"He doesn't want to scare you off, he's terrified you're going to run," he says.

"Is that what he said?" I ask, turning in my seat.

"Not in so many words, but I know my brother. Also to protect you. Reid is like that. I know he cares about you a lot, Summer. I've never seen him with any girl the way he is with you."

I wring my hands, not knowing what to say to that. "I don't like being lied to."

"He didn't really lie," Ryan says, defending him.

"Semantics," I mutter.

"You're so cute when you sulk," he teases.

"I'm glad you think so."

We arrive at Ryan's apartment, and walk up the stairs. "Since we're having a deep and meaningful, you going to tell me what happened with Xander the night he got into that fight?"

"Was I even at the bar that day?"

"Yes," I growl. "I know you know what happened. You guys gossip like old maids."

Ryan rubs his hand over his blond hair, making a sound in his throat. "Raptor has friends, they aren't fans of ours. Whenever we run into each other, let's just say shit doesn't always turn out well."

"Raptor?" I reply, scoffing.

"Yeah, that's what they call him in the ring."

"What do they call Reid?" I ask as he unlocks the door and waits for me to enter.

"Vengeance."

I stop in my tracks. "Why am I not surprised?"

"Want a juice box?" he asks, grinning.

"You guys got me juice boxes?" I perk up at the mere mention of them.

"Reid did," he says, opening the fridge.

"Apple?" I ask in a hopeful voice.

"Of course, and apple and blackberry." He smiles, throwing me one.

"Bloody hell, how can I be mad at him when he does cute and thoughtful things like this?" I grumble, stabbing the straw through the hole.

"Someone's easily pleased," he says, his eyes sparking with amusement.

"Was that a sexual innuendo?" I ask dryly.

"No, but it could be one," he chuckles.

"Let's watch Catfish," I say, walking over to the couch.

"You love this show."

"Yeah, cos it's awesome," I say in a matter of fact tone. I get comfy on the couch, just as Reid walks in, Jade in tow. She has tears pouring down her face, and she's sniffling dramatically.

"What's she doing here?" I demand, my hand twitching.

Jade walks towards the bathroom and Reid sits down next to me. "She was crying and crying, I couldn't just leave her there."

I glance at Ryan, and then back at Reid. "So... What? She's staying the night here?"

"What? No!" Reid says, taking my hand into his. He rubs my fingers while my hand lays there non-responsive like dead weight.

"Right. I'm going home, you deal with Miss I-Can-Cry-On-Cue," I tell him.

"For fuck's sake, you're not going anywhere, Summer," he says, sounding like he thinks I'm the one in the wrong here.

"I don't share well, Reid," I whisper so only he can hear.

"And I don't expect you to," he says, his eyes searching mine through his thick dark lashes.

"No, I think that you do. I get it, she's a link to your brother, and I'm not asking you to give that up. But there have to be some kind of boundaries."

"She doesn't usually act like this. Look, my baby brother loved her, he wanted to marry her. What am I meant to do?" he asks, distress flickering across his face.

Hating seeing him like this, I get up and walk to the bathroom. I tap on the door once before I enter. Jade looks genuinely upset, her tear-stained cheeks blotchy.

"Finally, some real emotion," I say wryly, leaning against the door frame.

"Yeah, well. I don't want to lose Reid and Ryan. They were meant to be my brothers one day," she says, her throat scratchy.

"Why did you kiss him?" I ask straight out.

Her head comes up sharply. "I was losing him, and I was desperate. I didn't plan it, it just happened. It was a mistake. I'd never do that to Reece," she says softly, and I actually catch a glimpse of the real Jade.

"Look, I'd never tell Reid to stay away from you, but we need to get a few things straight first."

133

She looks suspicious. "Like what?"

"You do not manipulate Reid into doing whatever you want, using guilt as a tool," I tell her, my eyes showing just how serious I am.

"What? I don't do that!"

"Shut up and listen. If those frosted lips, or any other body part even come close to Reid..." I trail off, letting my evil grin get my point across for me.

"I won't, I promise. He doesn't want me anyway," she tells me, wiping her tears away.

"As long as that's understood. Come on, let's watch Catfish," I say, walking out of the bathroom and back to Reid.

He looks worried. "Everything okay?"

I nod, pressing play on the show and smiling as he wraps me in his arms. Jade walks out a few moments later, and silently takes a seat. Reid nibbles on my ear. "Thank you."

"I have my moments," I say into his chest.

CHAPTER THIRTEEN

"Dad, there's a customer and I don't know anything about motorcycles to be of service," I say, peeping my head into the back office. My dad flashes me a grin and stands to his full height, scratching his beard before walking out.

I've spent the whole day helping him out in his bike shop. It's feels good to spend some extra time with him, and I can tell he enjoys having me around, too. It's a win-win situation. He's hinted at me working here full time with him, but truth be told I know nothing about bikes except that I love being on the back of one.

I'm not going to complain about the eye candy that walks in here, though, because damn, I never even knew this town had so many hot men. After two guys hit on me this morning, my dad put up a sign that says 'the discounts only apply to men that *don't* hit on my daughter.' I couldn't help laughing.

His store is having a huge sale right now, hence the large amount of customers today. I haven't been much help apart from ringing up a few orders, and ordering a few parts on the phone. I also vacuumed the store because there was nothing else for me to do.

On my break I walk to the deli across the road and get dad and me some food for lunch, and we sit in the office eating together. To other people this might seem like a normal, everyday moment, but to me it's times like these I dreamt of as a child. Spending time with my dad, joking, hanging out. I don't think I've stopped smiling all day.

"How's things with Reid?" he asks after we finish up lunch.

"Good," I say, a smile playing on my lips.

"I heard you're coming to the fight."

"Yup."

"You sure you okay with all of that?" he asks, studying me.

I shrug both shoulders. "Comes with the package that is Reid Knox, right?"

He suddenly looks uncomfortable, shifting nervously.

"What, dad?" I ask warily, pursing my lips.

He clears his throat, once, twice. "You're being safe, right, I mean. I assume your mother had chats with you, but I just wanted to make sure…"

I choke on my bottle of water. "Oh my god, dad!" I start laughing uncomfortably. "We haven't… that is… We haven't had sex yet."

My dad's eyes widen, looking surprised. He exhales and gives me a crooked smile, now looking both relieved and pleased.

"That was awkward," I mutter to myself.

"You can talk to me about anything, Summer, you should know that," he says quietly, rubbing the back of his neck with his hand.

"Thanks, dad."

"Xander mentioned how you reacted to seeing his mother," he says after a moment.

Now it's my turn to shift uncomfortably. "Yeah, I mean, I spent my whole life listening to mum blame her for you not being around. So it's kind of wired into me to feel weird around her. Mum hated her, and I guess I kind of feel like I'm betraying her by even considering being friendly with Daria."

Dad sighs, looking tired. "She was wrong to put that on you, just as I was wrong for messing up in the first place."

"I'll try, okay? I don't want Xander to not be able to have his own mother over because of my grudge. And if it wasn't for her I wouldn't even have Xander, and he's the best brother I could've ever wished for. So I guess everything happened for a reason," I tell him. I don't want dad feeling guilty over the past anymore. I love my mother, but she's gone, and I have a new life now. A new family. I will never forget her, or her memory, but I can't keep holding on to the hate she tried to instil within me.

"Your mother might have had her faults, but she raised a good girl," he says, looking proud.

I blush a little at the compliment. "Thanks, dad."

"We better get back to work," he says, standing up.

"How did you get into the underground fighting thing? I mean, you run it, right?" I ask him as we walk out.

"I'm one of the organizers, yes. I used to fight myself, Summer. It kind of just went from there," he says.

"Who taught Reid to fight?"

"As kids, Reid and his brothers did karate, they're all black belts. Two years ago, he found a trainer and I helped him, too. Xander, Dash, Ryan... They can all take care of themselves. We teach a few of the younger boys, too. Harlen and his friends," he says.

"I've met Harlen," I say, remembering the guy from the bar.

Dad chuckles. "Yeah, he told me about that. He was a little smitten with you, I think."

I stay at the shop until closing, peering out the window when I hear a rumble of motorcycles. Four men stop in front of the shop, and get off their bikes. Dad sees them and grins, instantly unlocking the door and walking out to greet them. After a few masculine displays of affection, I can hear them chatting and laughing while I grab my jacket and switch all the lights off in the store.

"Dad, can you lock the door?" I call out. Dad grins and walks over, locking up. Then he puts his arm around me and walks with me to the bikers.

"This is my daughter, Summer. Summer, these are my friends, Red, Dax, Bade and Henry," he says, gesturing to each one as he says their name.

"Hello," I say shyly, offering them a smile. A few grunts of hello ensue.

138

"She's beautiful," the one named Dax says, grinning. He looks to be in his mid-twenties, with hazel eyes. His dark hair is shoulder length and has a slight wave to it, and he's wearing a blue bandana on his head.

"I know. Now keep your eyes to yourself," dad mock growls. The men laugh good naturedly. They're all wearing the same cuts, so I assume they're a part of a MC.

"I'm going to head home, dad," I say, giving him a hug. I smile and wave to the bikers before getting into my car.

As I drive home I decide to drop by Reid's and say hello. He has an hour before he starts at the bar, and I know he's been training all day. He must be exhausted. His fight is tomorrow night, and I think I'm more nervous than he is. I knock on the door, rolling my eyes when Ryan opens it wearing nothing but a pair of boxer shorts.

"Expecting someone else?" I ask dryly, leaning on the wall.

Ryan grins, then looks a little uncomfortable.

"Oh, god, what am I interrupting?" I cover my face with my hands.

"Nothing yet," he says, smirking.

"Reid?"

"Not home yet, should be here any second, though."

"So, you aren't going to invite me in?" I say, my body shaking with laughter.

Ryan scowls and hesitantly opens the door. "Tag by himself?"

139

"Hired a new girl, so it's less strain now," he says, closing the door behind me. I can hear giggling as soon as I enter the living area, and gape when I see not one, but two women sitting there. I send Ryan a look that says 'you sly dog, you'.

"Do you want me to tell them to go?" he asks, frowning.

"No, no. Don't worry about me. I'll head into Reid's room."

"You sure? You know you're more important. Family is more important," he says, looking conflicted.

"You don't need to kick them out on my behalf. I'll go wait in Reid's room. Enjoy yourself," I say, kissing him on the cheek because he is just that sweet.

I make myself welcome in Reid's room, burying myself under the black comforter. When I hear Reid's voice saying, "What the fuck, Ryan? At least go into your room!" I start laughing. Reid opens the door, his face brightening as soon as he sees me lying in his bed.

"Fuck, you're a sight for sore eyes, beauty," he says, kneeling at the bed. He's wearing a pair of track pants and a black wife beater, and he looks seriously fucking hot.

"I missed you, so I thought I'd come see you before work," I say, leaning over for a kiss.

"You look so sexy in my bed," he says huskily, moving closer for another taste. He sucks on my bottom lip, pulling away too soon. I make a sound of complaint, earning me his signature grin.

"I'm going to have a quick shower. Stay right where you are," he says, leaving the room. I flip over and sigh into Reid's pillow. Reid and I haven't had sex, and he seems to be content with taking things slow. I, on the other hand, want him.

Bad.

I'm thinking up seduction techniques when Reid walks back in, dressed in only a towel. I sit up in bed, my eyes devouring him. His arms have the perfect amount of muscle, not too bulky, and his chest is toned to perfection. His stomach is full of sleek lines and ripped curves, and as rivulets of water drip down his abs, I swallow hard, my mouth suddenly parched.

He clears his throat and my eyes quickly dart to his. "I forgot my clothes to change into," he says, sounding slightly sheepish.

"Reid?"

"Yeah," he says in a low tone.

"Can I touch you?" I ask in a soft whisper. He doesn't reply, but takes the few steps between us, reaching the bed. I sit up on my knees, so my face is level with his chest. I place a soft kiss on the top of his ripped stomach, feeling his muscles tense the second my lips make contact with his skin. I lift my hand up tentatively, tracing the lines of his abs and running my fingers down his chest, our eyes staying locked together. He watches me through heavy lidded eyes, the blue shades darker than usual. I sink my teeth into my bottom lip, and Reid inhales deeply at the action. In a swift movement, his large hands grip my hips as he lifts me off the bed, and puts me down on the floor so I'm standing. His gaze is so intense, so probing.

"Are you sure you want this?" he asks, the low timbre of his voice thick and rough. The sound turns me on even more.

The word 'yes' barely leaves my mouth, when he takes my face into his hands, and kisses me hungrily. His tongue begs entrance, his rough moan penetrating the air when I open and let him in.

I can't get enough of him.

His taste.

His passion.

He starts kissing down my neck, trailing hot, wet kisses that leave me gasping. I don't think there's anyone that can kiss as well as Reid Knox. If this is a preview for more things to come...

Reid pulls away to lift up my top. His intense gaze rakes over my black lacy bra, and a growl of pleasure sounds deep in this throat. He unbuttons my jeans, and slides down the zipper. Licking his full bottom lip, he slides his thumb to the back of my jeans, and gently tugs down, until they sit just below my ass. My panties are plain black cotton, as I wasn't really expecting anything to happen between us tonight. I feel shy for a moment, until Reid says, "You are the most beautiful woman I've ever laid eyes on."

I wriggle a little until my jeans fall to the floor, and I'm left standing in front of him in just my bra and panties. He traces the tattoo on my hip with a long finger, reading the words aloud. "Be careful who you trust, the devil was once an angel." His head comes up sharply, a curious glint in his eye. Before he can say anything else, I lean forward and drop his towel with a flick of my wrist. I gasp as I take him in, naked in all of his glory. Strong, powerful thighs, lean hips and... Holy shit, he's even bigger than I thought. I bite my lower lip, my gaze touching on his abs, chest and shoulders before reaching his amused eyes.

"Wow," I say, my vocabulary leaving me. Reid leans closer, so our bodies are touching. We both moan at the contact, and I blush at his arousal pressed firmly against me. He is rock hard, velvet over steel.

"I think he likes me," I say, flashing an innocent look at Reid.

"I know he does," Reid answers hoarsely, walking me back to the edge of the bed, pushing me gently so I'm sitting. When he drops to his knees in front of me, I lick my lips nervously. The gesture makes Reid lose his last ounce of control, as he leans closer and captures my lips in a demanding kiss. I run my fingers through his hair, pulling gently as he takes my mouth. He licks, bites and tastes, until I'm begging for more.

"Please, Reid," I whimper, as he pulls my panties down, taking his time.

As soon as the words leave my mouth, Reid lifts my legs over his shoulders and starts to lick and kiss up the inside of my inner thigh. When he reaches my core and starts to slowly lick me, I shudder with pleasure. Reid moans, and knowing that he enjoys tasting me so much heightens my desire. He pays special attention to my clit, licking and sucking, causing me to squirm. Tangling my fingers in his hair, I lift my hips up, grinding against his face, trying to get as close to him as I can. Warmth soon pools in my lower belly, and when he sucks on my clit once more, streams of pleasure shoot up my spine, blinding me with its intensity.

"Reid," I call out, panting as wave after wave washes over me, my thighs trembling. Reid doesn't stop until the last tremor leaves my body, and I sag back onto the bed. That was amazing.

No - earth shattering.

Reid lifts his face, our eyes locked together as he slowly wipes his mouth with the back of his hand. Okay, that was fucking hot. When he stands, his huge length is pointing right at me, and sorely in need of attention. I grab his hand and pull him down so he's lying on top of me.

"I love your taste," he rumbles, licking his lips. I lift my head to kiss him, opening my legs so his hips align with mine. I reach down and take him into my hand, sliding the tip up and down my wetness.

"Are you sure?" he asks, his tone pure sex.

"Yes, now," I say urgently, moving my hands and digging them into his muscled back.

Reid takes over and slides into me slowly, watching me the entire time.

"Fuck," he curses, pulling back once, and then sliding all the way in. "Are you okay?" he asks, his voice sounding strained.

"Yeah, don't stop."

"Beauty, so wet for me," he whispers as he starts to move, grinding his pelvis against mine, rubbing against my clit with each thrust. The man knows what he's doing, that's for damn sure. He kisses me passionately, and I revel in his taste, his scent, his body. Everything about Reid draws me in. He lifts my thighs up, thrusts again, the penetration deeper. Reid makes a sound deep in his throat, and my eyes widen when I feel another orgasm cresting. I've never come twice before, and I find myself lifting my hips in rhythm with his, desperate for more.

"You're almost there, beautiful, I want you to come with me," he says, rubbing my clit with his finger.

"Reid," I gasp as the pleasure hits, consuming me. Reid moans and shudders on top of me, thrusting harder.

"Fuck, fuck, fuck," he says as he finishes inside of me. When we're both spent, he leans down and tenderly kisses my forehead, my brow, my nose, and then finally my lips.

"You okay?" he asks softly. I nod, giving him a sated smile.

"Look at you, swollen lips, sex hair, naked under me. Fucking perfect, Summer. How did I get so lucky?" he whispers. I pull his face down, kissing him on his jaw, over his scar. For once he doesn't pull away or flinch.

"It was perfect," I tell him, kissing him on the lips.

"We didn't use a condom," he says.

"I'm on the pill."

"I'm clean," he says.

"Have you had sex without a condom before?"

"Once," he says.

"Oh."

"Never felt as good as with you, Summer. I didn't even know it could be this good," he says, leaning his forehead against mine.

"Flattery will get you everywhere." I kiss his neck, and gasp when I feel him getting hard inside me again. "Holy shit."

"See what you do to me?" he says, his lip curving.

"I can feel it."

"You were made for me," he says, rolling his hips.

I push his shoulders as he rolls onto his back for me. "Let's test that theory, shall we?"

*****

"Weren't you supposed to go to work?" I ask, laughing.

"Shit," Reid says, pulling his phone out of the drawer. "Luckily Tag was there."

"Yeah, and the new girl."

"Yeah," he says, giving me a strange look.

"What?"

"Nothing. I'll go talk to Ry, gimme a sec," he says, kissing me once before leaving. He walks back in a few moments later with two juice boxes, putting one down on the table. The other one he opens, shoving the straw in and then handing it to me.

"Thanks."

"You staying the night?" he asks, looking hopeful.

"Sure. I'll just text Xander and let him know." He smiles with his eyes, and a little quirk of his lips.

"You want anything?" he asks, tilting his head.

"Just you."

CHAPTER FOURTEEN

After the perfection that was last night, I expected to wake up to one of a few different scenarios. Perhaps morning sex, breakfast in bed, or Reid's smiling face looming over me. Any of those would have been acceptable. What I didn't plan to wake up to, was Reid sitting there, staring at the wall, a pensive look on his face.

"Morning," I tell him, my voice thick. He glances down at me, and gives me a slight smile that doesn't reach his eyes.

"What's wrong?" I ask, sitting upright.

He rubs his hand down his face and purses his lips. "Don't worry about it, I'm just being stupid."

"Tell me."

"Come here," he says, moving me closer so I'm resting back on his chest.

"Reid," I say, letting my tone let him know that I'm serious.

"You want the truth?" he asks.

"No, lie to me, please," I say dryly, rolling my eyes.

"Fuck me," he mutters.

"What's wrong?"

"Okay, I'll tell you, but don't throw this in my face just for being honest," he says, sounding reluctant.

"Fine."

"I thought you were a virgin," he blurts out, holding my body in place so I can't move away.

"I never said I was a virgin," I say slowly.

"I know, but you're so innocent, and young, and you didn't say otherwise, so I just assumed…"

"Young? You think girls my age haven't had sex before?" I ask, the pitch of my voice going higher in disbelief.

"No, it's not that…"

"You think I'm a slut?" I gape.

"For fuck's sake, I didn't say that," he growls.

"You think I'm a slut for not being a virgin at nineteen?" I can't believe this shit. "How old were you when you lost your virginity?" I ask, scoffing.

"You're taking my words and twisting them, Summer," he says, exasperated.

"So that weird look on your face, that was because you were upset that you weren't my first?"

He lifts both shoulders in a shrug. "I just thought you were, that's all I'm trying to say."

"And the caveman in you wanted me to be?" I guess, gritting my teeth.

"Summer…"

"Well, there goes my morning after glow," I grumble, jumping out of the bed naked, and looking around for my clothes.

"And this is why I don't have relationships," I hear him say. I instantly spin around and stare him down.

148

"I'm sorry, what? This doesn't have to be a relationship, you know," I tell him, crossing my arms over my chest. His gaze lowers to my breasts and stays there.

Suddenly the door bursts open and Ryan walks in.

I scream.

He yells, and then puts his hands over his eyes. "Ryan," I hear Reid growl.

"I... uh... just wanted to say that I made breakfast," Ryan rambles, still standing there.

"Ryan, you can leave," I say.

"Yeah... Um... Okay." He finally walks out and closes the door behind him. I can hear his hyena laughter echoing down the hall.

"You didn't lock the door?" I ask, gaping.

"Apparently not."

Ignoring him, I wrap a sheet around myself, grab my clothes and walk to the bathroom. I have a quick, hot shower, brush my teeth with the spare toothbrush in the cabinet, and run my fingers through my hair so it doesn't dry knotty. I put my jeans back on, commando, and my bra and top from last night. I walk into the kitchen, my face flushing when I see Ryan standing there, grinning.

"I hate you," I grumble, heading for the stove.

"If you hate me then you don't get the bacon and eggs," he says, his tone laced with amusement.

"I'd like to see you try and stop me." I give him a hard look, taking a plate and serving.

"So you finally gave Reid a piece, hey," he says casually, drinking a juice box. Looks like my addiction is catching on.

"A piece? Who says that anymore?"

Ryan laughs.

"And how did you know we hadn't already?" I ask, buttering some bread.

"Aren't you going to toast that?"

"No."

"Why?"

"Hungry," I say, putting the egg and bacon on the bread and making a tasty looking sandwich.

"Reid's my twin, there's little I don't notice," he says, watching me take a bite.

"Who has the bigger penis?" I ask, wanting to shake him up. Of course Reid decides to walk out at that moment, scowling. "Well, if it isn't Mr. Old Fashioned," I grumble into my sandwich. Like an olden day lord pissed off because he found out his wife was a soiled dove on his wedding night. The thought makes me giggle. *I am so funny.*

"Our cocks are equally large," Ryan answers, chuckling.

"Did you think I was a virgin?" I ask Ryan.

He laughs harder. "No way, not with the way you move on the dance floor. Hips don't lie."

I blink twice, and then crack up laughing. Reid shakes his head at our antics, but I can see the smile on his lips that he can't stop from forming.

"Nothing is sacred in this house," I muse, finishing off my breakfast. Reid walks past me, gently tugging at a lock of my hair, before grabbing a plate and piling it with food.

"If you think you're going to get away with that as an apology, you have another thing coming, Reid Knox," I tell him, washing my plate and putting it in the dishwasher. I do the same for the other few plates and cutlery left in the sink. I spin around to find him leaning against the table, eating a piece of bacon with a smirk etched on his face.

"What's with the smirk?" I ask. I look around to see Ryan has left the kitchen.

"You're fucking hot when you're angry," he says, licking his finger.

"The way you act sometimes, you better get used to it."

"Ditto."

"I'm going home, I'll see you later," I say, walking past him. Before I can get out of his reach, he pulls me back by the belt loop on my jeans. My back crushes against his chest, and my heart flutters as he pushes my hair to one side so my neck is bared and vulnerable.

"I'm sorry. Last night was perfect, okay? I didn't mean to ruin it," he whispers, nuzzling my neck.

"Hmm," I sigh.

"Do you forgive me, beauty?" he says, his stubble tickling my neck.

"I suppose," I say ungracefully.

"I'll make it up to you," he says, and then proceeds to whisper exactly what he will do to me in my ear.

"Forgiven!"

Reid laughs at my eagerness. "Okay, drive safe and text me when you get home. I'll pick you up before the fight." Shit, how did I almost forget about that?

"Okay," I say, not sure how I feel about the fight.

"You don't have faith in your man?" he asks in disbelief.

"I do. I'll see you tonight," I say, kissing him on the cheek. He slaps my butt as I pass.

Men.

*****

I walk into the house to find an unhappy looking Xander standing in the kitchen, his arms crossed against his head.

"What's wrong?" I ask, putting my bag down on the table.

"You weren't here so I haven't eaten any breakfast," he says, sulking.

I purse my lips. "What did you do before I moved in?"

"Well, there were usually girls lying about so one of them…"

"You guys are disgusting!"

"Or we had leftover pizza, or something," he says, shrugging.

"Fine, I'll cook you breakfast but you're washing up." I point my finger at him and pull out some eggs.

Xander hugs me. "Thank you."

My heart melts. I love my baby brother. "You're welcome."

"I need to talk to you about something." The hesitance in his voice has me glancing at him.

"What is it?"

"I was thinking about getting in the ring sometime," he says.

"You wanna fight?" I say, enunciating each word.

"Yeah, I don't want you to get all upset, but I'm a pretty good fighter, and I wanna do this," he explains.

"Okay. Why are you telling me this?"

"Dad said I needed to..." he clears his throat. "Run it by you."

I can't help it when laughter bubbles out of my mouth. "Dad said you needed my permission?" I say through bouts of laughter.

"You done?" Xander growls, not looking impressed.

"Baby bro. Do I wish you wouldn't fight? Yes. But it's your life and I'll be there for you no matter what."

He looks at me with a softness in his eyes that makes me believe in the saying 'everything happens for a reason'.

"Right back at ya, Summer," he says. I smile and face the stove, cracking eggs into the frying pan.

After I finish Xander's breakfast, I get changed, tidy up the house and then drive to the library. Grabbing my assignment file, I walk inside and take my usual table.

"You're back," a deep voice says. I lift my head and stare into the eyes of the mysterious guy who sat next to me the last time I was here.

"You stalking me?" I tease. His lip curves as he sits opposite me, same as last time. He pulls out a thick text book, and I read it upside down.

"You're studying law?"

"Guilty."

I wince. "Looks painful."

"Trust me, it is. How about you?" he asks, gesturing to my folder.

"Nursing at Tafe." He tilts his head and smiles. I return to my assignment, wanting to get at least a quarter of it finished today. My phone vibrates and I pull it out of my pocket to see a text from Reid. I realize I never texted him saying I was home safe, so I send a quick reply saying I'm studying at the library.

"Boyfriend?" the stranger asks.

"You ever going to tell me your name?" I counter.

He grins cheekily. "Silas."

"Nice to meet you, Silas, I'm Summer, and yes, that was my boyfriend."

"All the good ones really are taken," he answers, but he doesn't look let down in the slightest, so I know he's just teasing. We spend the rest of the time in silence, until it's time for me to leave.

"Bye, Silas," I say as I pick up my folder.

"Bye, Summer," he says, not looking up.

By the time I get home I have an hour until Reid comes to pick me up. I jump into the shower, and then walk to my room with dripping wet hair. Wrapping a towel over my head, I stand naked in the corner of my room, staring at my wardrobe. What am I meant to wear? I settle for a pair of low riding skinny jeans and a tight black sweater. I put on my favourite pair of battered combat boots, because they're comfortable and flat, and they look pretty badass too. I blow-dry my hair and iron it so it's dead straight. A little mascara, powder and bronzer and I'm done.

"Summer!" Xander calls through the door.

"Yeah, come in."

He opens the door, looking excited and dressed casually in jeans and a white T-shirt. His shoulder length hair is pulled back at the nape of his neck. "You ready?"

"Yeah," I say, smoothing my hair with my fingers.

"You look fine. Reid's on his way," he says, bouncing on his feet.

"I'm glad someone's excited," I say as I dab some lip balm on my lips. I grab my phone and slide it into my bra, ready to go. Reid arrives ten minutes later, not looking his usual self. He looks like Reid when I first met him, tightly wound and brooding.

"You okay?" I ask him, wrapping my arms around his torso.

"Yeah, I get a little anxious before a fight," he says, which is understandable, I guess. Xander takes his own car, and I jump into Reid's.

"Summer," says a feminine voice from the back seat. My head spins around faster than the chick from The Exorcist, as I turn and see Jade.

"What are you doing here?" I ask, surprised.

"I've never missed a fight before, you think I'm going to miss one just because you're in Reid's life?" she says, staring down at her manicured nails. Fucking

Reid. A little warning would be nice. Reid slides into the driver's seat, and obviously feels the tension because he snaps, "Not today, alright."

The ride is silent and tense, and I stare out the window the entire time. Is he always like this before a fight? If so, I'd rather stay at home and watch Catfish. We arrive at a different location than the last fight, and it looks more crowded this time around. Reid steps out the car, and walks around to my door, opening it for me. He's dressed in a pair of shorts and a hoodie, which I assume will be coming off when he enters the ring.

"You okay?" I ask him softly. Jade opens her own car door, huffing about something or the other.

"Yeah, I'll be fine. Just… just stay with your brother, Ryan, and your dad, and stay where I can see you, okay?"

"Okay," I say, clutching my jacket and pulling it tighter.

"I'm serious, Summer, I want you in my line of sight."

"Okay."

We walk up to the entrance, and the man standing at the door lets us through, jumping the line. I ignore the looks a few of the women give me when Reid puts his hand on the small of my back and leads me in. When I see the huge caged octagon, I swallow hard. This place looks scarier than the last one.

I look at Reid to find him already looking at me, taking in my reaction. I attempt a smile but I'm sure it comes out more as a grimace than anything. He takes my hand in his, threading our fingers together. I take comfort in the gesture. Surprisingly, Jade steps up next to me, flanking my other side.

I spot my dad, my brother, Dash, and Ryan standing in a group, talking amongst each other. Reid squeezes my hand as we approach them. Dad immediately comes over and kisses me on the top of my head, and then pulls Reid aside, for what I assume is a pep talk. Another man walks up and joins them.

"Who's that?" I ask Jade.

"Reid's trainer," she answers. I notice her eye Xander, which makes me bristle.

"Don't even think about it," I say in a sing-song voice, my eyes still on Reid.

"I'd think you'd be happy, at least I'd back off Reid," she says.

I tilt my head to look at her. "Reid sees you like a sister. And as I'm sure you know, Xander is my brother."

Who I'm not willing to share with you, either.

I hear a few cheers so I look to see what the commotion is about. A bulky man dressed in a pair of shorts stands on the other side of us, a small posse surrounding him.

"That's who he's fighting?" I drawl.

"Yep. Daniel "Devil" Lanchester, in the flesh. He's kinda cute, huh," Jade says, nudging me with her elbow.

"What's with the nickname thing? Kinda silly, isn't it?"

Jade shrugs. "I don't know who started it but everyone has one. Maybe it's safer not to use a real name, not like these are sanctioned fights."

"Yeah except you still know the guy's real name," I say, shaking my head in confusion.

Jade shrugs, her attention going back to Xander. Yeah, like that's going to happen. "Oh, look. Your real competition's here. Haven't seen her here in a long ass time," she says sweetly, looking out into the crowd.

"What?" I have no idea what she's on about.

"Hey, sis, you ready?" Xander asks as he steps up next to me. Dash comes up behind me and wraps his arms around me.

"Ready as I'll ever be. Hey, Dash."

"Hey. You smell good," he says, sniffing me again.

"Hey, Ry."

"Hey, babe, come stand next to me, and don't move, okay?" he says, looking serious. His lips are pursed and stare unwavering.

I grin. "Did Reid threaten you?"

"He needs to be focused so we need to do our part on this end," he says.

"Well, don't worry about me, I'm not going anywhere," I say as I stare out at the crowd. The warehouse is filling up with even more people, and I start to feel a little anxious. I see Reid approach and run into his arms.

"Beauty," he murmurs, I can hear the smile in his voice.

"You gotta head up there, Reid," Ryan says, rubbing the back of his neck. Reid nods sharply, and takes a step back so he can remove his hoodie. Underneath is a white singlet, which he pulls off as well, leaving him bare-chested, and left in nothing but a pair of low slung shorts. No wonder people pay so much money to watch these fights. He wraps his wrists and hands, smiling up at me once he's done.

"Plenty of time for that later, Summer," he says, amused at my obvious ogling.

"Looking forward to it."

"Stay-"

"With Ryan, I get it. I'll be right here, okay. Just concentrate on the fight."

"That's my girl," he says approvingly, giving me a quick kiss before he heads to the centre of the Octagon. A man introduces Reid and his opponent, which is met with alternate cheers and boos. I start to wring my hands as I watch them both warm up a little, jumping up and down and stretching.

"He's going to be fine," Ryan tells me.

"Summer, stop fidgeting," Jade says. She looks calm and collected, then again, she's been coming to fights with Reid since he started this whole thing. Dad and Xander move in even closer, close enough that they can talk to Reid if need be. I'm happier being further back. I see Dash shifting on his feet, anticipating what's to come, and Ryan's intense gaze on his brother. I look back to see Reid and Daniel face one another, as the referee stands between them, talking. After a few moments of this, he knocks their gloves against each other twice and they both take a step back.

Then it begins.

The cheers are so loud that I wince, trying to block them out. As I catch a glimpse of Reid's expression, I can tell he's in the zone. His face is blank, and his eyes are hard, calculating. Apparently that doesn't stop his gaze from darting to where I'm standing, if only for a second. Ryan curses when he sees it, and takes a step closer to me so he's directly behind me. I know he doesn't want Reid to worry, even though I think they're all over reacting. I walked through the last fight, alone and in a pair of stilettos and I managed just fine.

Lost in my thoughts, I don't even pay attention to the fight, and a sudden cheer makes me snap to attention. Reid throws a punch to Daniel's head, and I turn to look at Ryan. Ryan grabs my shoulders and spins me back so I'm watching the fight. Reid and his opponent are now hugging each other, or at least that's what it looks like to me. Reid brings up his knee with force and throws a few more punches. How long does this go for, exactly? When Daniel gets in a kick to Reid's stomach, I reach back for Ryan's hand and dig my nails into his palm. Ryan brings me closer, and puts his arm on my shoulder.

I look around for a few seconds, watching people cheering, screaming, and jumping up and down. They're all so excited, so blood thirsty, when all I want to do is cry. I look back just in time to see Reid take him down to the floor, and I hear Ryan say something about a takedown. Reid practically straddles him and pounds into his face. When I see blood flowing from the other man's mouth, I start to feel a little nauseous. I face Ryan, not wanting to watch anymore.

"It's almost over," Ryan says, putting his hands on my shoulders.

Well, thank goodness for that.

What feels like thirty minutes later, the cheering turns to roars and they hail Reid the winner. My dad runs up to Reid, and checks him over for any injuries. Ryan leads me closer as Reid exits the Octagon. Forcing my feet to move, I watch his every step until he reaches me. I lift my hand to his cheek, frowning at the cut on his eyebrow. A few drops of blood drip down, but other than that he doesn't look too banged up. His chest heaves with his heavy breathing and I put my hand over his heart.

"Hey," I say.

His lip twitches. "Hey, beautiful."

"Let's take you to a doctor."

"No need, I'm fine."

"Your eyebrow!"

"You're going to be a nurse, you can stitch it up," he says, grinning. He smells like sweat mixed with his spicy cologne. Surprisingly, it doesn't smell bad at all.

"I'm still on the theory work!" I say, my voice going a little higher. No way could I stitch that up.

Reid chuckles at the look on my face.

"Reid!" I hear my dad call. "Doc will stitch you up."

"Who's your Doc?" I ask, looking around.

He winces, the poor man must be in pain. "Not one. Doctors we have on call for the fights. Why

161

don't you go wait with Ryan and I'll meet you out front?"

"Nice fight, Reid," Jade says, walking up to us.

Reid nods. "Almost there."

"Almost there," she whispers back, exhaling deeply.

"I'm going to get a doc to fix me up," Reid says, kissing me on my head. He gives Jade an undecipherable look as he walks off. Jade is scowling, her eyes following Reid.

"What is it?" I ask her, knowing something is up.

"Nothing," she says shortly. "Come on, let's go."

"Summer! Let's go!" Xander calls out. I follow the group outside, wondering what the hell is going on right now.

"You coming home with me?" Xander asks.

"No, I'll wait for Reid with Jade," I say.

"Ryan, you waiting here with them?" Xander asks him.

"Of course," Ryan replies, a scowl appearing on his handsome face.

"Okay, I'll see you at home then," he says, kissing me on the cheek. "Look after her. Precious cargo right here," Xander says before walking to his car.

I can see my dad smiling, looking proud. I roll my eyes.

"Dad, come over tomorrow for dinner," I say when he comes over to say bye.

"What are you cooking?" he asks, his eyes flaring with interest.

"Whatever you want," I reply, smiling.

"You know me, I'll always want meat and potatoes."

"Meat and potatoes it is."

"See you tomorrow, baby girl," he says, pulling me in for a warm hug. I turn to see Jade watching us interact, a wistful look on her face.

"I better be invited," Ryan adds, leaning on his car. The wind keeps blowing his hair into his face.

"Of course you are. Jade, you can come too," I tell her. She's not so bad after all, when she tones down the melodramatics. Jade looks surprised at the invite, hell, I surprised myself.

I look up from my phone, seeing Reid walk out towards us. His steps are hurried, and I can see his fists are clenched. What the hell happened? He pins me with his gaze, now close enough that I can see his eyes. They soften as they rest on me. "Let's go home, beauty."

"What happened?" I demand.

"Nothing," he lies. I know he lies because he looks away as he says nothing, not maintaining eye contact.

"What. The. Fuck?" I growl when I notice that he has pink lipstick stains on his neck. He's wearing a hoodie again, but they still don't completely hide them. I ignore Reid, my heart shattering, and walk over to Ryan's car, getting into the passenger seat. I'm not going home with that bastard.

"Summer..." Reid calls out, stalking to the car. I lock the door. Ryan sticks his head in the driver's side, looking confused.

"Will you take me home?" I ask him, my voice breaking. Ryan immediately hops into the car, and

163

closes the door, pressing the central lock so Reid can't get in.

"What's wrong?" he asks, looking baffled.

"What's wrong?" I repeat, sounding a little hysterical.

"Calm down, Summer," Ryan demands.

Reid stands next to the window and knocks on it. "Open the door, Summer," he says, sounding a little frantic.

"Reid has fucking lipstick all over his neck!" I say to Ryan, turning my back on Reid so I can't see him.

"Reid would never cheat on you," Ryan says confidently, trying to placate me.

"Yeah, so some bitch's lips just fell on his neck?" I can hear Jade and Reid talking to each other in heated tones.

"Why don't you just ask him? I'm sure there's an explanation."

"You driving me, or should I call a cab?" I ask him, my voice low.

"Fuck," he curses. He gets out the car and says something quietly to Reid. Reid pushes Ryan out of the way and hops into the driver's seat.

"For suck's sake, Summer, I didn't kiss anyone," he says, anger and worry flashing in his eyes.

"I'm pretty sure that speaks for itself," I say, looking straight ahead.

"Summer, look. She wanted me, she tried. I told her I was with you, and it was serious."

"That seems to be a common occurrence for you, right? Girls jumping at you while you remain the innocent victim," I spit.

He rubs his hands down his face in frustration.

"Who was she?" I ask him through clenched teeth.

"The doctor. She's kind of my ex. The one I broke up with just after Reece died," he says. His voice is low and sad, but I can't deal with both his pain and mine right now.

"So, you failed to mention that the doctor was your ex, your serious ex," I say, hurt and confused.

"I haven't seen her at one of these fights in a long ass time. This is the first one she's been to one since Reece. I didn't expect her to be here," he explains, his gaze locked with mine. "Look, I have a lot of baggage in my life. I don't wanna scare you away with all this shit. I want you to be happy, Summer, not have to worry about all this drama in my life. You're a good girl, you don't need to be around this shit. I wanted to keep you away from it, separate. So yes, I left a few things out," he admits.

"Why did you break up?"

He clears his throat. "Reece died, she was the doctor at the fight."

And she couldn't save him. Surely he didn't blame her for that?

"That wasn't her fault," I say quietly.

"I know that. I just pushed her away after that. We weren't meant to be together anyway."

"How do you know that?"

"I never felt for her even a quarter of what I feel for you. This intense, all-consuming need to be around you all the time, to protect you. I can't stop thinking about you, even when I'm sleeping I dream about you. We never had anything like that."

I look out the window, wanting a break from the conversation, to see Ryan and Jade have left in Reid's car. I didn't even hear the car drive off.

"Why is she still in there?" I ask, gesturing to the warehouse.

"There's another fight going on."

Well, that explains all the cars still in the parking lot.

"Can you take me home, please?" I look at him, and see that his eyebrow is nicely stitched. My gaze drops to his neck, where he's attempted to scrub off the lipstick but there are still smears of it where he missed a spot.

"Okay. Were you okay during the fight?" I can tell he's treading very carefully, trying not to get me upset.

"Ryan looked after me," is all I say. I look at his knuckles on the steering wheel, which are red and swollen.

"Will you come home with me?" he asks, sounding unsure.

"I think I'll just go home," I reply, shifting in my seat.

"You know I need to be near you after a fight," he says, his voice pleading.

"Why don't you stay at mine?" I offer.

He exhales in relief and nods twice. "Okay." He rests his hand on my thigh, his long fingers spread out.

"I'll stop by mine and grab some clothes," he says.

"You sure you're okay to drive?" I ask. I'm pretty sure I saw him take a few kicks to the stomach.

"I'm good."

When we arrive at his apartment Reid parks and runs inside to get some clothes while I wait in the car. I drum my fingers on my thigh, thinking over everything that I'd learnt tonight. I don't expect Reid to come without a past, without his own baggage, but this is getting a little ridiculous. One question is foremost in my mind.

What else is Reid Knox hiding?

And does it matter? As long as he's good to me, and faithful, can I take any curveball thrown my way? Reid enters the car, pulling me from my thoughts.

"You okay?" he asks, his hand on the keys.

"I'm fine," I say a little shortly.

"Right." He turns the key and starts the engine. He runs his other hand along his scar, looking like he wants to say something.

"I need to know you're in this with me, no matter what. I know I'm going to fuck up sometimes, but I'll always try and fix things. I'll never hurt you intentionally, Summer. I just need to know you aren't going to run. You can't run," he says, and I watch his Adam's apple bob as we swallows.

"Where am I going to run to?"

His eyes dart to mine before he replies. "You know what I mean. If something happens you can't handle, you're going to want to run from my bed, from me."

"Reid-"

"I just need to know if you want this as much as I do," he says. And there it is, the question I was just asking myself.

Apparently I take too long to answer.

"I see," he grinds out.

"Reid-"

He makes a dismissive sound in his throat, and keeps his eyes on the road.

"Are you going to listen to me? Or just be a dickhead?" I snap, losing my patience.

He doesn't reply, his jaw set.

"I want you. But you need to let me in more. You think I like finding out all of this shit from other people? Or from the lipstick on your neck? How would you feel if this situation was reversed? If I was caught with an ex of mine that you never even knew existed?"

I ignore the growl that escapes his lips and continue. "My point exactly."

"Tell me about your exes," he demands.

"Well, there are only two. I dated Liam for a couple of months, he was my first boyfriend. Then I dated Quinn for about a year. We broke up a month before I moved here."

"Who did you lose your virginity to?" he asks boldly, earning a glare from my direction.

168

"Quinn, and he's the only boy I've slept with other than you."

"Not a boy, beauty," he grumbles.

"Man," I correct, rolling my eyes.

"Where can I find this Quinn?" he asks in a suspiciously calm tone.

"Reid," I say, trying not to laugh but failing.

"What?" He shrugs his broad shoulders.

"So, this is the first time we're going to make love after a fight," I say huskily, changing the subject.

"Who says that's what we're going to do tonight?" he asks, playing coy.

I sigh dramatically. "I thought I was in for a treat tonight, my man winning his fight, adrenaline pumping through his body..." I trail off.

Reid grins widely, showing his straight white teeth. "Be careful what you wish for, beauty."

"Why? Cos I just might get it?" I bat my eyelashes at him.

"Just hope you can handle it," he teases, his lips curving into a crooked grin.

"Oh, I can handle it," I scoff, leaning over slightly and running my hand up his thigh.

He shakes his head at me, and as he parks on the grass in front of my house, I can feel the anticipation building. He walks around the car and opens the door for me, and I step out and stare up at his handsome face. A little battered, but handsome all the same. I smile and put my hand out, which he takes into his. He closes the car door, and locks it with a press of a button. Hand in hand, we walk to the front door.

Before I can even open the fly screen door, Xander pulls the door open, grinning when he sees us.

"I was wondering what the hell happened to you two, I just rang Ryan," he says, stepping back for us to enter.

"You okay?" he asks Reid, giving him a once over.

"Yeah, I'm good," he answers, slapping Xander on the back.

I pull Reid towards my room. "Night, bro!" I call out.

"Night. I'm heading out," he says.

I spin around. "Where are you going?" He just smiles cheekily and walks out. He locks the door behind him.

"Stop fussing over him," Reid says, cupping my ass with his large hand.

"I don't fuss over him," I lie.

"I'm going to take a shower," he says, pulling off his hoodie. I don't miss his wince, and I know that he's in pain, no matter how much he tries to deny it.

"Wanna join me?" he asks in a deep low voice.

"You sure you're up for that?" I ask.

He glances down at his semi hard on. "I think so."

"I meant, are you sure you're not in too much pain?"

"I will be, if you don't take care of it," he says, stifling a smile. He pulls off his top, and then his shorts, standing before me looking like a slightly battered Greek god.

I sigh as I stare at his body.

Sexiest thing I've ever seen. Who knew such perfection existed in real life? In books, maybe. Or in movies. But in real life?

"You going to stare at me all day, or you going to get naked and join me?"

I bite my bottom lip, and start to undress. I try for a slow, sexy seduction, but end up having to lie down on the bed to shimmy my jeans off. Once I'm fully naked, Reid stalks towards me and bends at his waist, gripping my hips and throwing me over his shoulder.

"Be careful, Reid!" I plead.

"I'm fine, Summer," he says, carrying me to the bathroom. Yeah, he is.

He puts me down on my feet, his arousal rubbing against my body as he releases me. Turning on the shower, he tests the temperature first, before lifting me in. I moan as the warm water hits my body, and at the promising look in his eyes. I stand up on my toes and kiss him slowly, a sensual tease. His tongue darts inside my lips, deepening the kiss as his hands roam my body. When his thumb swipes over my nipple, my body jerks in pleasure.

"I want you," he growls, pulling his mouth from mine.

"You have me."

He lifts me up in the air, and I instantly wrap my legs around him. "You sure you're okay?"

"Nothing's going to stop me from taking you. Want you too bad," he says before his mouth is on mine again.

"Then take me," I gasp as he pulls his lips away, only to move them to my ear lobe, nibbling. He

171

moves a hand down between us, and strokes me gently. He makes a husky sound in his throat when he feels just how ready I am for him.

When he slides into me with one firm thrust, a curse escapes my lips and exquisite pleasure consumes me. My back slams against the tiled wall with each thrust of his body, and I wrap my arms around the back of his neck, holding on. His lips return to mine, his tongue mimicking each thrust. I slide my fingers through his wet hair, tugging on it as my body erupts with waves of pleasure. A whimpering sound escapes my lips as he lowers his head to suck a nipple into his mouth, heightening my orgasm. He bites it gently before he pulls back, our eyes connecting. I watch his face as he finishes, the expression of ecstasy turning me on.

Reid pulls out and kisses me tenderly, his soft lips showing me how much he cares. We finish our shower, taking turns washing each other. He turns the water off and gets out first, taking a towel into his hands and holding it out for me. I step out and he wraps me up in it, kissing me on the nose. I look up at my man and sigh in contentment as he dries me with a towel.

Best. Shower. Ever.

CHAPTER FIFTEEN

"That's fourteen dollars, thanks," I tell the gentleman I'm serving. He hands me a fifty and I give him his change.

"Finally slowed down," Tag says, coming up next to me. We had a two hour long rush, the place was packed.

"Yeah. You can go have a smoke break, if you want," I offer, knowing he must be dying for one right about now.

"So, dating the boss and giving out orders, huh," he teases, his eyes playful.

"What?! Tag, I was just saying..."

Tag chuckles, pulls out a pack of cigarettes from the pocket of his jeans and heads outside. I can't help but stare at his jean clad ass as he departs. Buns of steel.

"Quit staring at my ass, Summer!" he calls out, not even turning around.

I'm just finishing cleaning up the bar when Jade walks in. I do a double take when she walks behind the bar, and starts grinning at me knowingly.

"You're the new chick?" I ask, my eyes flaring.

She laughs. "Yeah, and please don't be mad cos I need this job."

I lift my shoulder in a shrug. "Tone down your crazy and I'm sure we'll get along fine."

"Consider it toned down. What happened the other night after the fight?" she asks.

"Someone's nosey," I huff, cutting up some lime for the tequila shots.

"No, seriously."

"We fought, we made up. I had no idea the doc was his ex. I didn't even see what she looked like."

Jade gives me a head to toe once over. "You're way hotter than her."

I roll my eyes.

"No, I'm serious. You're all hips and boobs with a tiny waist. I've heard the guys talk about how hot you are."

"Are we bonding over the mutual dislike for Reid's ex?" I ask, stifling a laugh.

She grins evilly. "Yeah, I think we are."

Jade looks cute today, her blonde hair is tied up in a high pony tail and her makeup consists of lip gloss and mascara. Her tight jeans and black top show off her slender figure.

"Were you just checking me out?" she teases.

"Wow, what did I miss?" Tag says, wiggling his eyebrows at us.

"How come no one told me Jade was the new girl?" I ask, looking at each of them.

"I thought you knew," Tag says with a shrug. He runs his hands over the stubble on his cheeks before saying, "Ryan hired her."

"How's your daughter? I have a present for her in my car."

Tag's face lights up. "She's good. So smart. I'm pretty sure I have a genius on my hands."

"Her mum must be smart then," I tease, laughing when he pulls on my pony tail.

"Where's your man today?" he asks me.

"At the gym with Xander and dad."

"When's the next fight?" he asks.

"No idea." I look at Jade expectantly.

"Hey, I don't know either. You should ask your dad," she says.

I pull my phone out of my bra, and call Ryan.

"Hey, babe," he answers.

"Are we still doing dinner?" I ask him, hoping he says yes.

"Yeah, I'll be there in an hour."

"Okay."

"Bye."

We both hang up.

"You're going out to dinner with Ryan?" Jade asks, her eyebrows rising.

I frown. "Yeah, why not?"

"Isn't it weird?" she asks, pursing her pink lips.

"Ryan's my best friend." What's the big deal? I don't really care if people don't get our relationship.

175

We're friends, really good friends. Friendships like that are hard to come by.

"What does Reid say?" she asks, leaning against the bar.

"Reid knows Ryan and I are close." He acts like we annoy him but I know he's happy we get along so well.

She makes a noncommittal sound which just pisses me off. I'm about to tell her as much when a group of customers walk in.

An hour passes quickly, and soon Ryan walks in to pick me up. He's dressed in dark worn jeans and a long sleeve black sweater. His light hair falls across his forehead, and his baby blue eyes are warm.

"You ready, babe?"

"Yeah, give me a minute." I walk to the staff bathroom and change clothes, then re-apply some make up. I spray myself with my new Vera Wang perfume, and I'm good to go.

"Okay, let's go." I say as I walk out, my bag in hand. I say bye to Tag and Jade, and walk out side by side with Ryan.

He pulls out of the car park. "What do you feel like eating?"

"Creamy chicken and mash potatoes," I answer instantly.

He chuckles deeply. "I know just the place."

"So, what's new with you?"

"Nothing, same old. Work hard, play hard."

"We all know you play hard. I was at your place the other night," I tease.

"Oh, like you're all innocent. Oh, Reid! Reid!" he imitates, causing me to burst out laughing, my face turning a little red.

"Are you blushing? You're the only girl I know that still blushes."

"Yeah, right!"

"I'm serious. Most girls are forward these days, they don't blush or get shy."

"Maybe the women you hang around."

"What does that mean?"

"Maybe you should try picking up chicks somewhere different. In a library, perhaps. I assure you the women who frequent there would probably be blushers."

"Stereotype," he says in a sing song voice.

I roll my eyes. "Maybe so, why don't we put that to the test sometime?"

"You're on. What did I do with my time before you moved here?" he asks playfully.

"Have more sex?"

He thinks it over. "You're probably right. And try to keep an eye on Reid, but now you're here for that."

"Ha!"

"I think you're the only person he will listen to."

"I think you're exaggerating," I reply.

"Oh, please. He's so pussy whipped," he says, then commences to make whipping noises.

"Mature, Ryan," I say, shaking my head and smiling.

"Seriously though, you're good for him, babe. I'm happy you're here," he says in a gentle voice.

"I can't handle your sweet, Ryan," I say, looking out the window.

"Don't get all hormonal on me," he says, chuckling.

"Aaand you're back."

"We're here, come on." He says, getting out of the car. I hop out and walk around to meet him.

"You didn't tell me you hired Jade," I say after we order our food and drinks.

"I'm sure I did," he says, looking around the restaurant.

"Scared of my reaction, Ryan Knox?"

His eyes snap to mine and narrow. "I had to hire her. She needed the money and she was my brother's girl. Was I a little worried how you would react? Maybe," he admits. "But it was also kinda fun, waiting to see what you'd do."

"I don't mind Jade, and it's your bar, you can hire who you want."

"Yeah, but I was hoping you would think Reid hired her, not me."

"You're evil."

"There's always an evil twin," he says in a creepy voice.

"Two in some families," I tease, poking my tongue out at him.

"Who's the babe?" comes a deep voice. I look up into the face of a muscular man with reddish hair and green eyes. He has a goatee and a slightly crooked nose.

"None of your fucking business. Leave," Ryan demands, his voice dangerously low.

"I saw you at the fight, you're Reid's bitch?" he leers, staring down my top.

I sit up straighter in my seat, pulling my top up as high as it can go.

"I'm next up against Reid," he says, sounding thrilled. Reid is fighting this sasquatch of a man? Fucking hell.

"Get the fuck out of here, before you regret it," Ryan spits out. His hands clench on the table, and his jaw is set stubbornly.

"You guys share this bitch, or what?"

Ryan stands up. I know this guy is just pushing him, obviously wanting Ryan to react.

"Ryan," I say, my eyes pleading with him. A guy calls out "Frank" and the sasquatch retreats, his smug chuckles permeating the restaurant.

"Stupid fuck," Ryan curses.

"Don't let him get to you. Let's try to enjoy our meal, okay?"

"Shit, I was worried about you, babe. If he wanted to fight I have no problem handling that, hell, both Reid or I could kick his ass. But then one of his asshole friends would have come up and started to harass you, I know how these assholes operate."

"Is that who Xander got into a fight with?"

"Not the same guys, but other fighters. There are some good guys who fight, then there are some dickheads like those, who go looking for fights and drama everywhere they go."

"He was scary," I admit.

Ryan scowls. "I'll never let anything happen to you, babe."

"I know that, he just looked like a serial killer."

Our food arrives and we wait quietly as they place down our plates.

"Thank you," Ryan and I both say to the waitress at the same time.

"Shit, maybe we are seeing too much of each other," he jokes, lightening the mood.

"Cos we're both polite?"

"Cos we're speaking at the same time. Even Reid and I don't do that, and we're twins."

"Sexy twins," I correct.

Ryan grins. "You're so good for my ego, babe."

"Trust me, your ego doesn't need any stroking, Ryan." I eye his food. "I want a bite."

"Of course you do," he says dryly.

"What you're like Joey from *Friends* now, you don't share food?"

"*Friends*." He chuckles. "We should watch that tonight."

"Let's. We should take home dinner for Reid, too."

Ryan gives me a taste of his steak, I give him a bite of my chicken. We finish up and then head back to their apartment, with a shitload of food for Reid. I wonder if he's even home yet. What I don't expect to see, as we walk up the stairs to the front door, is a woman standing there. Dark red hair and fair skin. I can't tell the colour of her eyes from where I'm standing, but I instantly recognise her as the woman from the bar.

"What are you doing here?" Ryan growls from behind me.

"I need to talk to Reid," she says in a stern tone.

"Reid's moved on, doc, you need to let him go," Ryan says, nothing gentle in his tone. I should have known she'd show up here at some point, because that's just how lucky I am. Ryan walks around her, his hand on my wrist, pulling me closer. While he unlocks the door, my gaze can't help but be glued to Reid's past, I never got a good look at her the first time around. She's a lot older than me, that much I can tell. She must be in her thirties, so older than Reid, too. Ryan shuffles me into the house, hesitating with his hand on the door. She's still standing there, and Ryan clearly doesn't want to just shut the door in her face. He looks at me and shrugs his shoulder.

"We can't just leave her standing there," I whisper.

Ryan looks at me quizzically. "You're a one of a kind woman, babe."

"Why?"

"Other women would throw her down the stairs then slam the door shut in her face."

"Great, now I'm thinking about it."

Ryan gives me a belly laugh. We're both saved from making any decisions about letting her in when we hear Reid's deep voice.

"What the fuck are you doing here?" he growls, and I cringe, because his tone is downright hostile.

"I wanted to talk to you," she says, sounding a little unsure. Ryan and I share a glance before we shuffle against the wall so no one can see us standing here listening. We're terrible, I know, but I could care less right now. Reid isn't much of a sharer of information.

"We have nothing to talk about, I told you the other night."

"Reid, I want you back."

Reid sighs, like he's put out. "And I told you that isn't going to happen. I love my woman, nothing's going to change that."

Wait, what? He loves me? I glance at Ryan, wide eyed, who is smiling his megawatt smile.

"You love her?" she says, her voice breaking.

"Yeah, I do."

"That young girl? Is she even legal?" I open my mouth, but Ryan pinches me, reminding me where we are.

"For fuck's sake, Mia. You need to go. I'm sorry, but don't come back. I don't need you ruining what I have, it's good."

"What does she have that I don't? We were amazing together in bed, fucking wild, so it can't be that."

And I'm back to thinking about pushing her down the stairs.

"We're done, Mia. Please go home, alright?" he says, his voice softening a little. I hear her heels clicking away. Ryan grabs my arm to pull me away from the door, but then we hear Reid speak.

"Enjoy the show?" he says. Luckily he sounds amused, not angry. He walks in and wraps me in his arms, placing his face in the crook of my neck and shoulder.

"Missed you today, beauty," he says, reigning kisses on my neck. He pulls back and kisses me gently on the mouth.

"Did you miss me?" Ryan asks, grinning.

"No," Reid answers playfully. "You two are trouble together, I swear," he says, shaking his head at us.

Ryan takes the plastic bag filled with food and puts it on the table. "Brought you dinner."

"Thanks, bro."

"Thank your girl," Ryan answers mischievously.

"I plan to," he says, fusing his lips to mine.

"Get a room!" Ryan calls out, heading into his own room.

"Ryan, don't come out of your room," Reid tells him and walks me backwards to the couch.

I hear Ryan say, "Kinky bastards."

"Wait, what are you doing?" I ask, sounding panicked. Reid smiles and sits me down. He removes my black flats, and then pulls off my jeans.

"I need to taste you, now," he says, the urgency evident in his breathy tone.

"Reid-" He kisses me, halting any objections. Taking my jeans and panties off, he kisses me until I'm breathless. Oxygen is trivial, all I need is his kisses to survive. When he pulls away to kiss down my neck, I'm panting. With no warning, Reid lowers his head

183

and attaches his mouth to my centre, his tongue darting inside.

I scream, not even caring that Ryan can hear.

CHAPTER SIXTEEN

"Is it true?" I demand.

"Is what true?"

"Are you not dating anyone because of me?" I ask, frowning.

"After what happened with Tina…" he trails off.

"Cos Tina was a bitch, you decided not to date anyone else?"

"Not for a while, I just wanted to make you my primary focus," he says softly. I love my dad.

"You don't need to put your life on hold, dad," I tell him, hating that he's doing this because of me.

He chuckles. "It's not some big sacrifice, baby girl."

"Okay, but you don't need to worry about me. And yes, Tina was a bitch, but I was selfish too. I shouldn't have been happy you dumped her. Did you love her?" I ask, suddenly feeling guilty.

When dad bursts out laughing, I know that no, he didn't love her. "You're too cute, Summer."

"Okay, but we're good, dad, yeah?" I say, letting my eyes convey what he needs to know. We're solid. I'm not going to push him away, the past is in the past, and I'm not going to be throwing any old demons in his face.

"Okay, baby girl," he says.

"I want you to be happy," I tell him, smiling at him fondly. "You know I still have all the money you sent me sitting in a bank account."

"Really? You didn't spend any of it?" he asks, frowning.

"No, I didn't want your money back then, dad. I just wanted you. I didn't know the whole story, so I thought you were just paying me off for being absent."

He closes his eyes and I curse myself for bringing it up. "Hey, I know it wasn't like that now. And now I have money saved away for a rainy day," I say.

"You want any more money you just gotta say the word, baby girl. I'm not hurting for it," he says.

"I know, dad, but I'm okay and I like working for my own money," I say.

He grins. "You're a good girl."

"I try," I say, satisfied.

"You going to feed me now?" he asks with a grin.

I laugh. "Of course, old man. Take a seat."

After classes that day, I head to the library to study. With a heavy sigh, I pull out my text book and highlighter, and get straight to work. After an hour or so, I look up when I hear someone pull out the chair opposite me.

"So we meet again, Silas," I say, amused.

Today, though, Silas doesn't seem to have an easy smile for me. In fact, he looks a little worried.

"You okay?" he asks.

"Yeah, why?" I ask, feeling suspicious.

"Just wondering." Hmm.

"What have you got today?" I ask him, glancing down at his own massive text book.

"Commercial law," he replies with a groan.

I grin. "Sounds so interesting."

"It's not. But it's all about the end goal, right. I'll be able to help people that need it," he says quietly.

"Help people how? By sucking their blood?" I say, giggling. "Okay, I'm sorry, no lawyer jokes. Even though I have a shitload of them."

Silas gives me an amused look, shaking his head at my antics. "You might need me one day. You know, to divorce your third husband or something."

"What are you trying to say?" I demand, gasping in mock outrage.

"Nothing at all," he says, smirking.

"Okay, I need to study so I'm going to ignore your presence for a little while. Don't take offence," I say, continuing with my work. After another hour, I'm done. I look over at Silas to see him chewing on his pen, brows scrunched in concentration. Not wanting to disturb him, I quietly pack my books and stand up to leave.

"Bye," he says, glancing up from his work for a sec.

"See ya," I say before I walk out. The sun hits my eyes as I exit the door, so I find my huge red sunglasses in the bottom of my bag and put them on. Xander calls these glasses my 'bug' glasses because they cover half my face. I prefer to think of them as my hangover glasses.

When I walk into my living room after an uneventful drive home, I'm surprised to see Reid lying down on the couch. His bare feet are hanging off the edge, and when I step closer I see he's wearing nothing but a pair of jeans.

Now, this is a sight I could get used to coming home to.

"This is a nice surprise," I say, sitting on the edge of the couch next to his hip.

"Hey, beautiful," he says, his voice thick. His blue eyes smile at me.

"Were you sleeping?" I lean over and nuzzle his neck.

"Mmm-hmm."

"Slide over, baby," I say, trying to wedge myself in. Reid chuckles and lifts me up so I'm lying directly on top of him, every inch of our bodies in contact. "Someone's happy to see me," I say, grinning. I grind my hips into his, earning myself a throaty moan.

"Always happy to see my girl," he says, smiling at me.

"Didn't you have work today?"

"Nah, Ryan said it's dead so there was no point going in."

"That was nice of him." I lay my head on his hard, warm chest. I run my fingers up his arm, feeling his smooth skin.

"How was class?" he asks, wrapping his arms around me tightly.

"Good, actually. I'm on top of everything," I say, stroking his chest absently.

"On top of everything, indeed." I roll my eyes at his lame joke.

"What are we doing tonight?"

When Reid stills, I look up into his eyes. "What is it?"

"Ryan told me what happened at dinner," he says, his jaw set stubbornly.

"Yeah, that guy's an asshole," I mutter.

"Yeah, he won't be bothering you again," he says, his voice sure and determined.

"What did you do?" I ask, frowning.

"Nothing yet, but I asked your dad to move the fight up," he says, sounding smug.

I sigh. "Reid, what's that going to accomplish?"

"No one disrespects my woman."

"Caveman."

"You love my caveman tendencies," he says, grinning.

"Only in the bedroom," I admit, earning me a deep chuckle.

"Seriously?" I hear Xander growl as he enters the lounge room. I sit up off of Reid and smile up at my brother.

"Hey, baby bro."

"We need to set some damn boundaries, sis," he says, looking put out. He opens the fridge and pulls out an energy drink.

"We aren't doing anything," I say a little defensively, my face heating.

Xander huffs and walks out, but not before I see the small smile playing on his lips.

I grin down at Reid, who I find is already looking at me. He looks... content. His eyes are soft, and I watch as he licks his bottom lip.

"You look happy," I think out loud.

"I am happy."

"Good," I say, leaning down to kiss his scar.

"My father did it to me," he says, his voice so low I barely hear him.

I sit up. "What?"

"Yeah, he was hitting my mother, and I tried to stop it. He said he wanted to teach me a lesson," he says, pulling me down against his chest once more.

"How old were you?" I ask, dreading the answer.

"Ten."

Tears pool in my eyes, as I imagine a young Reid Knox, standing up to his own father. "Your dad's in prison, right?"

"Yeah," he says, but doesn't elaborate.

"I'm sorry," I say, my voice breaking a little.

"Beauty," he croons, when he sees me getting choked up. "I've never been a good boyfriend," he continues when I don't say anything more. "I never thought I would be a husband. Ever. But after meeting you I think, maybe this time, I could be different. For you, I could be. I think I already am."

"You're perfect for me," I tell him, capturing his lips in a needy kiss.

"Fucking hell!" I hear Xander curse as he walks back in, ruining the moment.

"Next time we're going to my place," Reid demands, looking grumpy.

"Or you could just go into her room," Xander mutters, walking out the front door and slamming it shut behind him.

"Well, the coast is clear," Reid says, smiling against my lips. He runs his hand up the back of my thigh, causing chills to erupt all over my body. I reach my hand down to stroke him, just as we both hear a knock on the door.

"Maybe they'll go away?" he says, looking adorably hopeful.

Another knock. Louder this time.

"Impatient bastards," he mutters, sitting up with me still on him.

"I'll get it," I say, lifting a leg down onto the floor.

"No, you won't, you lie here and relax, I'll get it," he says, kissing me on the nose before jumping off the couch.

"Put your shirt on!" I say, picking it up and throwing it at him.

He looks amused. "Why?"

"Humour me," I say, rolling my eyes. He flashes me a boyish grin and puts his shirt on, walking quickly to the door when more knocking commences, louder this time. I hear him open the door, and then an angry, "What the fuck are you doing here?"

I get up and follow him to the door, my eyes flaring when I see Mia standing there. And she's not alone.

Next to her is a little boy.

One who looks exactly like Reid.

Blond hair, blue eyes and a cute little pair of lips.

I look at Reid, who is staring at the boy in shock. "No way," he says suddenly, looking freaked out. When he stands there and does nothing but gape, I tell them to come in. We all walk into the living area and sit there awkwardly. Mia sits the kid down next to her on the couch.

Moments ago, I would have sworn my life was perfect.

"He's yours," Mia says, looking worried, but also a little smug.

Feeling like I'm suddenly intruding I say, "I'm going to leave you guys alone for a second." I stand up until Reid pins me with a glare.

"Sit, I need you here, Summer."

"No, let her leave, she doesn't have anything to do with this," Mia says, her eyes narrowing to slits.

"She has everything to do with this," Reid sneers. His face softens when he turns to me, his eyes pleading with me to stay.

"Why don't I take…" I trail off, realizing we don't even know the kids name.

"River," she replies stiffly. She looks like she doesn't want me near her son, but she also desperately wants to talk to Reid alone.

"River, why don't you come with me? I'll show you my Ninja Turtle toys," I say, ignoring the curious look from Reid and the hostile one from Mia. Even though she's throwing daggers my way, and probably thinking up ways to kill me, she gives me a slight nod, letting me know it's okay to take him.

River grins at me, so I walk over and awkwardly lift him into my arms. Reid broke up with Mia two years ago, so he must be a year and a couple of months old. He feels heavy in my arms, and I lift him higher, holding him closer. I don't wanna drop the poor kid. I can feel both their eyes on my back as I walk to my room, pushing the door open with my foot.

I sit River in the middle of the bed, then shake my head, thinking that that can't be a very good idea. I put him on the carpet, and then reach under the bed for my favourite childhood toys. I pull out the plastic container, and peep inside, looking for my favourite Donatello figurine.

"Uh huh!" I cheer as I find it. Making sure nothing can come loose on him, I hand him over to River. River stares at him, blinking furiously. Then he picks him up and throws him as far as he can, which ends up being about a metre.

Poor Donatello.

"Not a TMNT fan, huh? I don't think we can be friends, kid," I say, grinning. River walks over and pulls out a doll, making a face. Then, ignoring the toys, he walks to my side table and starts pulling my TV remotes. Reid walks in as I'm trying to gently pry the remote from his pudgy little hands. I look up at him, and I know my eyes are full of questions.

193

"She says he's mine. And looking at him, I can't really deny it," he says, his brow furrowing.

"Okay," I say. I mean, what else am I supposed to say? It is what it is, right?

"Are you okay with this?" he asks me, and I want to scream.

"Yeah, this is just how I imagined my day going," I say sarcastically. I pick up River, and hand him to Reid. Reid holds him away from his body, as if he has no idea what to do with him. And I guess he doesn't.

"Why'd she keep him away from you?"

"She said I wasn't in a good place after Reece died, and she was protecting River," he says.

What a bitch.

"You should go, Reid, get to know your son," I say, giving him a sad smile.

"Summer-"

"Go, Reid, I was going to take a nap anyway," I say, trying to sound convincing.

"Okay, I'll be back tonight," he says, kissing me on the lips before pulling away. He hesitates at the door, turning back and watching me.

"I'll see you tonight," I say, forcing a smile.

"I'm so lucky to have you, beauty," he says softly, before walking away. I hear the front door close as they leave. Only then do I let my tears fall.

Reid doesn't come back to see me that night.

CHAPTER SEVENTEEN

Two days later I still haven't seen him. Sure, I haven't gone to his house either, but he's the one who said he would come to see me. He's been calling and texting every couple of hours, seeing what I'm up to, how I'm doing. Sometimes I reply, and sometimes I don't. I know he's getting to know his son, and it makes me feel like a bad person to hold that against him. He wouldn't be a good man if he didn't want to make up for lost time with his own child. I may be selfish, but I can't help how I feel.

I'm young, way too young to even consider having children yet. Not that I don't love and want kids in the future, because I do. But there are things I want to do first. Travel the world, drink too much, and be spontaneous.

Things that I can still do, but not with Reid.

Our lives are suddenly heading in completely different directions, and my emotions are all over the place.

I'm trying to keep myself occupied, so I don't become one of those girls lying in bed all day, feeling sorry for myself. Yesterday I spent the day with dad and Xander, and today after classes I go to the library to study. For once Silas is absent, and I find myself missing his company. I could use the distraction.

As soon as I walk into the bar, I want to scream at the looks of pity Tag and Jade are throwing my way.

"You okay?" she asks kindly, watching me with concern.

"I'm fine. Is Ryan back?" I ask her. Ryan had gone away with some woman for a few days, missing all the drama.

"Yeah, he's coming back tonight. I don't think he even knows what's going on," she says, scrunching her nose up.

"Reid didn't tell him?" I ask, surprised.

"Not something you really wanna say over the phone."

Ain't that the truth?

"Where do you want me?" I ask Tag. I know he's worried about me because he doesn't even respond with a sexual innuendo.

"Babe," he says gently, that one word holding so much meaning. He kisses me sweetly on the top of my head.

"I'm fine, really. So, my boyfriend has a kid." I shrug with fake nonchalance. "You have a kid, right Tag? Lots of men have kids," I say with smile that's all teeth.

"I think that smile's going to scare the customers off, you wanna do stock take?" he asks, frowning.

Hiding out the back sounds perfect. "Yes, please."

A couple of hours later, we are just closing up when Ryan storms in looking around. When his eyes land on me, I know it's me he's searching for. He takes me into his arms, giving me a warm hug.

"How you holding up, babe?" he asks, saying it softly so only I can hear him.

"I'm alright." I take in his familiar scent. "How was your trip?"

"It was amazing, but I wish I'd have been here with you instead. Why the hell didn't you call me?"

"It wasn't my place to tell you about your nephew."

"Okay, maybe so. But you're my friend and I always wanna be there for you. Especially when Reid couldn't be," he says, rubbing gentle circles on my back.

"I'm fine!"

"Sure you are."

"Ryan!"

"Come on, you and I are spending the night together," Ryan says, exaggerating his voice. I nod. Ryan is always good company.

"What's going on?" I freeze at Reid's voice. Ryan and I both glance up at Reid, who's standing there watching us. I notice several subtle emotions pass on his face.

"Summer?" he says, looking at me strangely. If he asks me what's wrong, I think I might scream.

"Hey," I say, stepping back from Ryan's hold.

"Come on, let me take you home. I wanna talk to you," he says, putting his hand out.

I take his hand, stepping closer to him. "We can talk, but I'm going with Ryan," I reply.

"You can see Ryan after," he says, his voice hardening.

"I just told Ryan we'd hang out. I haven't seen him in a few days," I say, pushing my hair back behind my ear.

"You haven't seen me either," he says, narrowing his eyes.

"Not my fault," I say, lifting my shoulder in shrug.

"So that's how it's going to be, huh? You aren't going to support me, be understanding about this?"

"Reid, I'll come see you tomorrow morning, how about that?" I say, trying to placate him. I'm not ditching Ryan just because Reid suddenly remembered he had a girlfriend.

"Mia was right, you're way too immature to handle this," he says to himself. That comment hits me like a blow to the chest. One thing I've learnt about Reid, his words can be cutting. He knows exactly what to say to hurt you the most. And he hit his intended mark with that one.

"Ryan, let's go," I say, my eyes still on Reid. Instead of shuttering my emotions, I let them show, but don't feel any satisfaction when he flinches at the pain I know is clearly displayed.

His face softens. "Summer-"

Ignoring him, I walk out into the car park looking for Ryan's car. When I spot his motorcycle instead, I grin. A ride on that will definitely improve my mood. I turn back and see Ryan and Reid talking, Ryan making angry hand gestures. Shit, the last thing I want is to come between them, I've never met siblings as close as those two. Reid walks out alone a few minutes later, a scowl etched on his handsome face. He storms up to me, where I stand waiting next to Ryan's bike.

"We need to talk," he demands, taking me by the elbow and pulling me closer to him.

"What do you wanna talk about?"

"I'm sorry I haven't seen you, or came back to your house like I said I would. Mia's been annoying the fuck out of me, and I've been trying to spend some time with River," he says, looking apologetic.

"I'm proud of you for stepping up, Reid, but I honestly don't know how this is going to affect us. I'm not trying to be a bitch, I'm just being honest. Mia is going to get in the way-"

"I won't let her!"

"She's your kid's mother, Reid. Shit's going to be different now," I say softly, looking at the ground.

He lifts my chin up with his finger. "It might be different, but it doesn't mean it's going to be any less amazing between us. I love you, Summer. I don't wanna lose you. I need you to be patient, and be there with me through this."

He loves me?

"Let's go, babe," Ryan calls out as he walks up to us.

Reid takes a helmet and puts it on for me. "You going to our place?"

"You going to be there?" I ask him.

He clears his throat. "No, Mia wants me to come over there and..."

I cut him off. "Right. Well, then yeah, I guess I'll be at yours."

Reid curses, and I hate the helpless look on his face. I hop on the bike and wrap my arms around Ryan. I see Reid watch us together and scowl. I wave my fingers at him, and then we're off.

*****

"Could you at least pretend to be enjoying my company right now?" Ryan says, throwing a piece of popcorn at my head.

"I always enjoy your company."

"You've been staring at the wall for the last ten minutes," he points out.

"Did you see River?" I ask him, curious.

"Not yet, I told Reid to bring him here tomorrow. I wanna go shopping first and get the little guy some presents. Kids love presents," he says, his eyes lighting up.

"You going to see Zara again?" I ask, talking about the woman he went away with.

"Maybe," he says, smiling mischievously.

I roll my eyes. "Your dick is going to fall off one day."

I laugh when I see him cupping himself and frowning.

"Touch wood," I say, grinning. He looks down at his crotch again, looking confused.

I burst out in laughter. "No, I meant touch something wood. You know, when you say something and you don't want it to happen, so you touch

200

something wood. Like a table or something, not…
that," I point to his penis.

"Oh." Then his eyes widen with realisation.
"Ohh," he says.

"Oh, indeed," I say, wiping away tears of laughter.

He chuckles. "You're so weird."

"Thank you for making me laugh."

"Anytime. Now you going to watch the movie?"
he asks, raising a brow.

"Yep," I say, in a much better mood now. Reid
told me he loved me tonight, and I didn't even get to
enjoy the moment. The truth is, I love him too.

More than anything.

I just hope we can work this out.

Dash and Xander drop by, and I laugh when I see
that my brother has gone to the grocery store and
bought all the ingredients for his favourite meal. He
actually brought them all to Ryan's apartment and
asked me if I would cook for him with puppy dog
eyes he knows I can't say no to. Dash looks hopeful,
too, his violet eyes smiling at me.

"Where the heck have you been, Dash?" I ask him
as I'm peeling potatoes.

"Around," he says vaguely.

"You hardly come to the bar anymore."

"Yeah, I've been a little distracted," he says,
looking down at his shoes.

"I'm always here if you wanna talk," I say softly,
studying him.

"I know, baby," he says, walking over and kissing me on the forehead. "You know when I first saw you, I was going to make a move on you."

"What? Really?" I remember him checking me out that first day, but that's about it.

"Sure, you're beautiful, loving, there's just something about you, Summer Kane," he says, flashing me a crooked smile.

"So, what happened?" I ask, nudging him with my elbow.

"I saw how you looked at Reid, you were done for, baby girl," he says, shaking his head at me. I blush, looking down at the potato. "I heard what happened. Didn't see that one coming."

"You and me both," I say, enunciating each word dramatically.

"Well, you know where to look if the two of you break up," he says, waggling his dark eyebrows.

"Ryan?" I joke.

"Ha-ha, very funny," he says. "You want some help?"

"Sure, you can cut up some tomatoes for me. Thanks."

"No problem. Don't think I can handle any more Dynasty Warriors with those two," he says, groaning.

I gape at him. "Dynasty Warriors is my favourite game. In fact, I'm the one who bought it!"

"That explains it," he says, his lip twitching.

I point at his chest with my finger. "See. You and I wouldn't have worked out."

"Cos I don't like that stupid game?" he asks, chuckling.

"Yes."

"Does Reid like it?"

"Reid *loves* it," I say.

"I'll bet he does," Dash says, his eyes twinkling.

"What does that mean?"

"It means I'm sure Reid likes anything you like, or at least pretends to. Hell, if you were mine, I'd play that stupid game, too, just to see you smile."

My eyes flare in surprise. "That was... really sweet, Dash."

He winces. "Yeah, let's keep that between the two of us."

We share a look. "Always."

CHAPTER EIGHTEEN

"I brought you coffee," Silas says as he takes a seat next to me.

"*You* are a lifesaver, I really need to get this assignment done," I say, grinning up at him. I take a sip of my coffee. Strong, just the way I like it.

"What happened to you?" I ask when I see his cut lip.

He touches his mouth with the back of his hand. "Just a scuffle."

"Let me guess, I should see the other guy?"

He chuckles. "Exactly."

"How's your assignment going?" I ask him.

"Almost done," he says.

"Lucky you," I grumble, highlighting something in my text book.

"You seem happier today," he observes. I haven't seen Reid in three days, but we've been talking a heap on the phone. I've been really busy with class and Reid's been busy with training, River and running the bar. I was in here yesterday and the day before, and so was Silas. We're kind of each other's unofficial study buddies.

"I feel happier today," I tell him. And I do. I've thought about Reid, River and Mia a lot since I found out the news, and I think that I love Reid enough to make this work. If he still wants me. I plan on heading to his house after this to talk, and move forward. Sure, I don't know anything about kids.

But I could be River's friend.

I could support Reid. It's not like he's asking me to act like River's step-mother.

I realise I've hurt Reid, and I haven't been there for him because of my own jealousy and insecurities.

First things first, I need to finish this damn assignment.

*****

The drive to Reid's apartment is filled with nervous energy. I park my car a little crooked, jump out and rush up the stairs. Ryan answers the door after several knocks. He smiles when he sees me.

"Hey, babe."

"Hey. Reid here?"

"He's at the park with River," he says, stepping back so I can enter.

"I'll wait for him."

"Good. He's been moody as hell, you two need to make up. For the sake of my sanity. Even Jade won't go near him," he says as we walk into the living room.

I sink down on the couch, and slip my thongs off my feet. "How's River doing?"

"Good. He loves me," he beams. He runs his hands through his hair, the blond locks falling right back into place.

"Loving the stubble, Ry," I say honestly, checking out his scruffy look.

"Really? Hmm, maybe I'll leave it," he says, a gleam in his eyes.

The door opens, and Reid walks in. He's holding River up in the air, the both of them smiling. Mia walks in behind them, and seeing me, lays a possessive hand on Reid's chest.

That one move has me seeing red.

I watch as Reid smiles widely as he sees me, putting River down carefully and practically running to me.

"You're a sight for sore eyes, beauty," he whispers in my ear, before he pulls back and kisses me on the lips.

"You're in front of your son, Reid," Mia scolds, her face going an unattractive shade of red. Reid ignores her and kisses me once more, soft and sweet.

"We need to talk, baby."

I nod. He trails his gaze over my face, as if memorizing each individual feature.

"I'm going to go then, Reid," Mia says sternly, trying to pull the attention back to her. Reid turns towards her, but only has eyes for his son. He picks River up and hugs him close to his chest.

"I'll come and see him tomorrow, alright," he says to Mia. "I'll go walk them out, Summer."

Ryan chuckles and I look at him, curious. "What?"

"Mia wanted to stay here and cook dinner for Reid tonight. She didn't expect you to be here."

I scrunch up my page. "She better get used to it."

He laughs again, clearly amused. "I should get some popcorn, watch how this plays out."

"You're meant to have my back! Some BFFL you are," I complain.

"What the fuck is a BFFL?" he asks, looking baffled.

"Best friend for life," I say. Duh.

"That term is so overdone. I'm more like your pole," he says after a few thoughtful seconds.

I blink twice. "Did you just call yourself my pole?"

"I did," he says, looking pleased with himself.

"A pole."

"Yes, a pole."

"Are you going to explain that, or just leave me sitting here with my 'what the fuck' face on?"

"I'm here for you whenever you need to lean on me. Like a pole."

I look at him for a few full seconds before I start laughing so hard, my stomach starts to hurt.

Ryan actually starts to look offended. "I'm pretty sure a BFFL isn't meant to laugh at you so much."

"What's so funny?" Reid asks as he walks in.

"Your brother is hilarious," I say, looking at Ryan again, and immediately erupting in another fit of laughter.

Reid loses his patience and lifts me into his arms, bride style. I'm still giggling when he lays me down on the bed.

"God, you're even more beautiful than when I last saw you," he says reverently, taking my hand in his and kissing my knuckles.

"I'm sorry I wasn't here for you, Reid. I was scared, and a little jealous, to be honest."

He instantly looks over and gives me his full attention. "Why would you be jealous?"

"You're connected to Mia now, for life, and she still wants you. I'm not your priority anymore, and I get that, your son should come first. I just couldn't help the way I felt, though. I went from being your everything, to you not even having time to come and see me. I know it sounds selfish," I say in a small voice.

"It's perfectly understandable, babe, I shouldn't have done that to you. I don't want you to feel as though you aren't important to me, because you are. I fucking love you, baby, there's nothing more important to me. Things will change, they will get better for us."

"How do you know?"

"When you love someone as much as I love you, trust me, beauty, it's going to work out," he says, a faint smile on his lips.

I smile back at him. "I love you too, Reid."

He's instantly on top of me, his weight pushing me into the mattress. "Say it again."

"I love you."

"Fuck," he says, resting his forehead against mine. "I don't want Mia. I haven't even looked at her that way, I guess I'm stuck with her cos of River. I do want to be friends with her, cos that's what's best for him. But it's you I love, you I think about all day long, you I want in my bed every night," he says, pushing his hips against mine.

I reach up and tangle my hands in his hair, pulling his lips down to mine. I fuse them together, needing to taste him. God, I've missed his touch so much. My lips part for him the second his tongue begs for entrance and he kisses me deeply, showing me with his lips just how much he has missed me. After he's had his fill of my mouth, he moves to my jaw line, and then down my neck, trailing wet kisses. I squirm, feeling a tug in my lower belly with each kiss, loving each sensation. He pulls me up into a sitting position, where he removes my top and my pink bra. He lies me back down flat on my back, where he continues teasing and torturing my neck and collar bone. A rough thumb swipes over my nipple, making my back arch off the bed.

What this man does to me.

His mouth trails lower, until he reaches my breast. One hand plays with one of my nipples, while he sucks the other into his hot mouth.

"Reid," I pant, when he nibbles softly. I can feel him smile against my breast. When his mouth heads further south, I'm trembling in anticipation.

"Go faster, Reid," I hiss, as he takes his time licking down my hip. He ignores me, and continues to worship my body everywhere but the place I need him the most. I'm about to lose it when he finally reaches my centre.

One minute later I'm screaming his name.

An hour later, I'm screaming it again.

*****

"Reid, I love you but if you try and make love to me again I won't be able to walk," I grumble as a large rough hand sensually touches my breast. My comment follows a masculine chuckle, and I can tell he's pleased. Caveman.

"Come on, I'll run you a bath," he says, standing up. I admire his taut behind as he walks out of the room. We had sex four times last night, each time more amazing than the last. Smiling widely, I reach out for my phone to check the time. Ten am. I don't have any classes today, but I work at the bar at three. Plenty of time. I relax into the bed, stretching my arms above my head. I pull she sheet up to my chin when I see Ryan storm in, smiling. He's bare chested, and wearing nothing but a pair of 'Family Guy' boxer shorts.

"Morning, babe."

"Seriously, Ry, boundaries," I say dryly. I glance down my body to make sure nothing can be seen.

He continues like I never spoke. "I had to sleep with my iPod on last night."

I blush profusely when I get what he means. "I'd say I'm sorry but that would be a lie."

Ryan laughs and walks to Reid's cupboard, pulling out a shirt. Huh, apparently it's not only women who do that.

"You stealing Reid's clothes?" I ask, brows rising.

"No. I'm stealing back my shirt," he says as he walks out. A beat later I hear, "Whoa, Reid, put some fucking clothes on, bro," and I can't contain my laughter.

"Bath's ready, baby," Reid says, standing at the door.

"Put some clothes on, poor Ryan."

210

"He sees the same thing in front of the mirror every day," Reid points out, and I laugh some more. He holds out a towel for me, and I stand butt naked and wrap it around myself. I squeal when he lifts me in the air, and carries me to the bathroom, putting me on my feet and pulling the towel away. My heart warms when I see a bubble bath all ready and waiting for me.

"Thanks, babe," I say, pulling him in for a quick kiss.

"I'll go make some breakfast, you enjoy your bath," he says, winking before he exits the bathroom. Smiling, I step into the bath tub, and sink down slowly. The water is just the right temperature, Reid knows I like the water really hot. I let myself soak until my fingers start to wrinkle and then quickly wash my body. I hop out and take my toothbrush, brush my teeth and brush my hair. Walking back into Reid's room, I pull out a T-shirt of his and put it on. It comes up to my mid-thigh, so I throw on a pair of boxers, too. Way too big, but will have to do.

The kitchen smells like pancakes when I walk in, and I grin at the twins, both standing in front of the stove. Reid smiles when he sees me, and quickly serves three pancakes on a plate. He drizzles it with maple syrup and places it in front of me.

"You look sexy in my clothes," he rumbles, looking pleased and a little turned on.

"You like me in anything."

"Or out of anything," he counters. We both grin at each other.

"Yeah. I'm going to go to work," Ryan announces. He kisses my head as he walks past and heads for his room.

"What are we doing today?" I ask Reid as I take a bite.

"I'm going to go see River, then I'm going to the gym. Why don't you come with me?" he asks, watching me closely for my reaction.

"I gotta work at three and I need to go home and get dressed," I say. Reid opens the fridge and takes out an apple juice box, placing it next to my plate. "Thanks."

"Beauty, I really want you involved with River, and I don't know how to do that if you don't wanna come and see him with me. I don't want you to push me away."

"Okay, I'll come with you. I'll take my car so I can leave to work straight from there."

He thinks it over. "Okay, sounds good."

"I'm going to hop in the shower," he says. He walks over to me and kisses my cheek. "Thanks for trying, baby."

I'm pretty sure I would try anything for this man.

An hour later, we're standing at the front of Mia's door. I'm wearing a black top, pants and ballerina flats. My hair is tied up in a high pony tail, and I'm wearing just a touch of makeup. I shuffle my feet, feeling completely out of my comfort zone. Reid touches the small of my back, and it helps a little. Mia opens the door, wearing what looks like clubbing attire. A halter neck white top, and tight black skinny jeans. She smiles brightly as she opens the door, but the smile drops the instant she sees me.

"What's she doing here?" she sneers.

Reid scowls. "We spoke about this, Mia."

They did?

After a few tense moments she opens the door, grudgingly letting me in.

"Where's River?" Reid asks Mia.

"He's having a nap," she says. So if Reid came here alone, him and Mia would what? Sit around and spend some alone time together?

Just fucking great.

We all sit on the couch, and no one says anything. "Well, this is awkward," I mutter under my breath.

Mia's brown eyes snap to mine. She hates me, I can see it in her eyes. We're saved by River's cries.

"I'll go and get him," Reid says, standing up and leaving the room. Leaving me alone with bitch face. Her phone rings, the ring tone Miley Cyrus's 'Wrecking ball." She silences it.

"You like Miley?" I ask her.

"Yeah, so what?" she says, a little defensively.

"No reason," I say in a sing-song voice. Some people are so touchy.

"So what, you too good for Miley?" I almost laugh at how crazy she sounds.

"What? No, I actually like this song. I don't understand why she gets to third base with a hammer in the video, but to each their own."

"You're not going to take Reid away from me," she says, scowling.

213

"You shouldn't scowl so much, you'll get more wrinkles," I say in a fake sweet tone.

"You little bitch, you know nothing about Reid, about what he needs."

I shrug with nonchalance. "I have him, you don't." Her face turns red with anger.

Reid walks out, holding River in his arms. He still looks sleepy, rubbing his eyes with his hands. He gives me a toothy smile when he sees me, and squirms from Reid's hold. Reid puts him down and he walks right over to me.

"Hi," I say to him when he stops in front of me.

"Hello," he says, and we both smile at each other. He's a cute kid, truly. Reid pulls out a huge box of blocks and places it on the floor.

"Wanna play blocks, River?" he asks his son.

River beams, and my heart warms. I sit down on the floor next to Reid, and take a pile.

Building towers with my man and his cute kid isn't the worst way I could spend my day.

CHAPTER NINETEEN

"I need four tequila shots, beauty," Reid calls out.

"Okay." I'm at work tonight with Reid and Ryan. It's been pretty busy all shift, and it's only starting to slow down now. I pour the shots and place them on the table, with packets of salt and cut lime.

"Thanks, baby, you wanna take your break now?" he asks.

"Yep."

"Okay, grab whatever you wanna drink." I pour myself a coke, waving when I see Jade walk into the bar. She sits down at a table and motions me over.

"Hey, what brings you here tonight?" I ask, taking a seat next to her.

"I need to get laid," she blurts out, and I choke on my drink.

"Give a girl a little warning before you say shit like that!" Jade is my only girlfriend around here, and we've never had any type of conversation like this before.

"I'm sorry but I haven't been with anyone since Reece and I think it's time."

"Wow, that's a long time."

"I know. So I figured I would come here because Reid and Ryan would screen whoever I was interested in. And if I end up in a ditch, you guys would know who killed me," she says casually.

"Alright, you aren't going to end up in a ditch. Isn't there someone you already know?"

I clear my throat when she looks towards Ryan and Reid. "Don't even go there."

She laughs. "Just playing with you. Is Xander here?"

"Yeah, don't go there, either."

"What are you to up to?" Ryan says, taking a seat.

"Jade's trolling for penis," I say, giggling.

Ryan doesn't look amused. "I'm sorry, what?"

A flush works up Jade's neck.

"She has needs, Ryan."

"Yeah, so don't wanna hear this," he says. I glance over at the bar and see a woman standing there, staring at Reid.

"Who's that woman trying to get Reid's attention?" I ask Ryan, almost wanting to laugh at her blatant attempts.

"Oh, that's Tilly. Everyone knows Tilly." He says this like it isn't a good thing.

"I don't know Tilly," I say dryly, taking in her frizzy blond hair and heavier set figure. She kind of looks like she's been electrocuted.

"Tilly's well known around town. She likes to go after taken men."

"Taken men?" I repeat slowly, surely I misheard.

"Yeah, she doesn't discriminate. Young, old, doesn't matter what they look like, either. She just likes them to be married or in a serious relationship," Jade adds.

"You're joking?"

"Unfortunately not," she replies solemnly.

"Likes sloppy seconds, does she?" I chuckle.

Jade shrugs. "Doesn't matter to her."

"No seriously, why would a woman want that?" I ask, genuinely puzzled. I try my best not to judge, but come on!

"My guess? Low self-esteem. Makes her feel good about herself that she managed to tempt someone that belonged to another woman. Usually a better looking woman than her."

"I don't even know what to say right now," I mutter as I watch her plump her breasts in Reid's direction. He doesn't even look her way.

"Yeah, best part is, she's married, but her husband is never at home, couldn't care less about her. I think he realized what he married, but it was too late, cos they have three kids. So he just leaves her to her own devices. So she's got extra time on her hands, and nothing better to do."

"Every town has a home wrecker," I say absently. "Her poor kids. They must be embarrassed as hell." I would be. Who wants everyone in town talking about their mother and the men she chases after just for a little desperate attention? "She doesn't care about age?"

"Nope," Ryan says. "She's been with a twenty one year old, last I heard." He's such a gossip, I love it.

"And how old is she?" I ask.

"Mid-thirties."

"Doesn't anyone tell her husband?" I wonder out loud.

"He's got something on the side, so don't think he really gives a shit about her."

Wow, lovely family. Once again, poor fucking kids.

"She also likes to kick up men's protective instincts by playing the victim, saying her man ain't treating her right and hinting of abuse, saying how bad things are for her at home," Jade says, taking my drink and taking a sip.

"And guys go for her? They cheat on their girls with her?" I gape.

Jade purses her lips. "She's easy. And strokes their egos."

I roll my eyes and divert my attention back to Reid. Tilly is now leaning across the bar and smiling a come hither smile. Reid ignores her, and I can't help but laugh. She turns to glare at me, and then starts to talk to the girl next to her, who also turns to look at me. She even points once. I grin, all teeth.

"They're talking about you," Ryan says, pointing out the obvious.

"I know."

He eyes me curiously. "I thought you were the kinda girl that would get in her face right about now."

"A tiger doesn't lose sleep over the opinion of sheep," I say, flashing Ryan a mega-watt smile.

Ryan lifts his head back and laughs. "You are something else, babe."

"Besides, my mother taught me to respect my elders," I say.

"What about him?" Jade asks, pointing at a cute guy standing at the bar.

Ryan shakes his head no. "Douche bag."

"Him?" she asks, gesturing to a cute blond man.

"He's a drug dealer," Ryan says solemnly.

"He is not!" Jade gasps.

"Hey, he's hot," I say, checking out a muscular tattooed guy.

"He has a wife and a mistress," Ryan immediately adds.

Jade puffs out a breath. "There's only one other attractive guy here tonight. The guy with the dreads."

"He has a pregnant girlfriend," Ryan says.

"You are such a liar, Ryan," I say, laughing.

Ryan shrugs. "You learn things about people when you work at a bar."

"What about Tag?" I ask, grinning.

Jade actually looks like she would consider it. "Guaranteed multiple orgasms right there."

"Definitely," I agree.

Ryan groans. "I don't wanna know." He stands up and heads to the bar to help out Reid.

"How long's your break?"

"Thirty minutes. Why? You need a wing woman?"

"Yes, actually, I do."

"Maybe you should ask Tilly." We both laugh at that.

"Seriously, Reid can't stop watching you. It's not like you're going to disappear," she says. I lift my head up to find him watching me. He flashes me a grin, which I return whole heartedly.

"Can I ask you why the sudden need to get laid?" When she instantly looks down, I know something is up. "What is it Jade?"

The colour drains from her face, but she tries to school her expression. "It's nothing, it's just time."

I don't buy it, but I let it go. "You wanna come to my house before the fight next week?" I ask, changing the subject.

"Actually, no. I'm not going to go to the fights anymore. It's not going to fix anything, if Reid beats Raptor or not. I'm letting it go, and he should, too."

Whoa. Something is definitely going on here. "Okay, but I'm here if you wanna talk, alright."

She looks relieved that I'm dropping it. "I'll remember that."

"I better get back to work. Look, why don't we go out sometime this week, and maybe you can meet someone," I offer.

She nods. "Sounds good. I'm going to head home."

"Alright, bye," I say.

I watch her walk out with the feeling that something isn't right.

*****

His name escapes my mouth as wave after wave of pleasure takes over me. Reid grunts as he slides into me one last time. I collapse onto my stomach, my face buried in the pillow. Reid pulls out of me and pushes my hair to the side, kissing the back of my neck. I lift my face up from the pillow so I can talk.

"Is it just me or does it get better every single time?" I ask.

He chuckles softly. "It's fucking perfect every time, baby."

"I thought so."

Reid lies down next to me, and rolls me over so I'm facing him. He lifts the sheet to cover us both, and snuggles towards me.

"I love you," he says, staring into my eyes.

"I love you, too."

"Do you? Or do you just love the three orgasms I just gave you?" he says, smirking.

"Both," I say sleepily.

"Sleep, baby," he whispers.

I fall asleep instantly.

CHAPTER TWENTY

"What's going on with Jade?" I ask Tag a week later, who is leaning in a sexy pose against the wall. Tonight is Reid's fight against the sasquatch guy from the restaurant, and even though I'm feeling a little under the weather, I'm definitely going to be there to support Reid. After this fight, he gets to fight the guy that his brother lost against.

Lost.

Died.

If I'm being honest with myself, isn't death a chance you take when you enter something like this?

"I dunno, she's been very quiet though," Tag says, frowning.

"Did you guys have sex?" I ask, grinning.

"What? No. Why? Does she want to?" he asks, grinning.

"Who doesn't, Tag?" I tease, winking at him.

He throws his head back and laughs. "No one, babe, no one."

"That's what I thought. You coming to the fight tonight?" I ask.

"Nope, got my little girl tonight. We're watching The Little Mermaid and eating popcorn," he says, smiling.

My heart melts. This tough looking guy with his shaved head, muscular build and goatee is such an amazing father. Goes to show, never judge a book by its cover.

"Don't swoon over me, girl," Tag says, his eyes twinkling.

"I'll try."

"Try harder."

"You're such a good father, I can't help it."

His eyes darken. "It wasn't always this way. I made some fucked up mistakes in the beginning." He turns and walks off.

Touchy subject, then.

"What are you doing here?" Ryan asks, frowning as he walks in.

"I know you guys need help for the rush, so I thought I'd come in for an hour or so."

"Reid wants you with him," he says.

"Reid can wait an hour without me."

Ryan doesn't look so sure.

"Relax, Ry."

"I can't help it, babe, it's an important fight," he says, rubbing his hands on his face wearily.

"I know, trust me, I know," I say quietly.

"Yeah, all I know is you better be there. Jade isn't going for some reason, but Reid doesn't care cos he just needs you there."

"So I've heard," I say dryly.

Ryan tucks a lock of my hair behind my ear. "Go home, babe, get ready. We'll come pick you up," he says.

"Alright," I tell him, but end up serving a few more customers and wiping down the bar before I leave.

A couple of hours later I'm dressed in light denim distressed jeans, a light pink V neck top and black boots. My hair is tied away from my face, and flowing down my back in a ponytail. Reid rang me and said he was going to the location earlier to warm up, so I'll be riding with Ryan. I hear a horn sound and rush to the front door, locking it behind me. Sliding into the car, I shoot him an amused look.

"Beeping the horn, really? If this was a date you'd be considered a douche."

"Well, I rang your phone and you didn't answer, and unlucky for you, but this isn't a date," he says, grinning mischievously. I watch as he reverses the car and pulls onto the road.

"Unlucky for me? Really? I've seen enough of the Ryan Knox charm to know how you operate."

"How I operate?" he asks, eyebrows rising.

"Yeah, flashing that charming smile of yours, your smooth lines…"

"Smooth lines?" he repeats, scoffing.

"Yep."

"Babe, all I need is this face and this body, not to mention what I can do for a woman in the sheets, and I'm pretty much good to go," he brags.

224

"So modest."

He shrugs. "It's the truth."

"You're pretty hot," I admit, a little reluctantly.

He laughs. "Of course you'd think so."

"I may be biased, though."

"Just a little," he says, squashing his thumb and index finger.

"I'm a little partial to those baby blues."

"You're perfect for Reid," he says, smiling at me with such warmth, I get a little choked up.

I clear my throat. "Where's the fight held?"

"Place you've never been before. It's a little further out," he says.

"Is Mia going to be there?" I ask.

"Probably. She's not the only doctor that comes out, though, so maybe not."

"Can I ask you something?"

He nods his head yes.

"Why wouldn't Reid stop fighting, now that he has River, I mean, wouldn't that seem more important?"

Ryan sighs. "He considered it. But it's only two fights left, and then he'll be done forever. He's come this close."

"I guess," I say, starting to feel a little anxious. I only hope he wins tonight.

The drive is about half an hour, and I'm surprised at the amount of people around the warehouse.

"Shit, there's more people here than the last two fights."

"Yep," he says, finding a secluded parking spot a little away from the crowd.

"He's going to be fine, right?"

"He's going to be fine."

"Okay, let's do this, then," I say, taking a deep breath.

The atmosphere is different tonight, it's thick and heavy. Filled with anticipation. I can see people holding up signs for both Reid and his opponent, some more creative than others. For the first time at a fight, there are seats around the ring. Ryan takes me by my arm, and I smile when I see familiar faces. Xander, dad and Dash. I hug all three men and then look around for my man.

"Where is he?"

"Out back, he'll be out in a minute," he says.

"Can I go see him?" I ask, my gaze darting.

"Just wait, baby," Dash says, pulling me closer to him.

Something's not right.

I sigh in relief when I see Reid walk out. He's shirtless, and a little sweaty, like he's already been fighting. I head in his direction, stopping when I see his face. He looks mad. No, not mad, he looks pissed. He raises his head and sees me, and I watch as his face goes soft right before my eyes. He reaches me in a few quick steps.

"What's wrong?" I ask quickly.

"Nothing, now that you're here," he says, pulling me against his warm chest.

"Tell me-"

"There was an incident, I took care of it. I gotta head up now. You know the drill, stand with Ryan," he says, lowering his face for a quick but passionate kiss.

"Love you."

"You too, beauty, you too."

He escorts me back to Ryan, and they have a silent conversation with their eyes. After a few moments, Ryan steps forward and hugs Reid. Reid grins, and pulls away, walking off with my dad and Xander.

"Why's everyone so tense tonight?" I ask Ryan so only he can hear. He doesn't reply, instead sets his hands firmly on my shoulders, and positions me so I'm standing right in front of him. The fight starts, and I watch as Reid and Frank circle each other. Reid throws the first punch, hitting him square in the face. I turn to look at Ryan, and then see a familiar face.

"Silas," I call out, waving my hand. I frown when I see his nose is bleeding, and his cheek is swollen. I step towards him, wondering if he's okay, frowning when I see the emotions on his face. He looks worried and unsure.

Worst of all he looks guilty.

Ryan turns to look where I'm looking and his face turns to stone. He walks over to Silas, and I follow quickly behind him.

Ryan lifts his hand and hits Silas, who instantly falls to the floor.

"What the fuck are you doing, Ryan?" I shriek, my mouth open in horror. I lean down onto my knees and put my hands on either side of his face.

"Are you okay?" I ask him, feeling panicked.

227

"How the fuck do you know him?" Ryan asks me in a tone I've never heard before.

"From the library," I say, confused. I turn to see Reid rushing towards me. A glance back at the ring shows a huge form lying unmoving on the floor. Shit.

I've never seen Reid look so terrifying before. His jaw is set, his fists are clenched and his eyes are cold as ice.

Unfeeling.

Impenetrable.

I gulp when he pins me with a scathing look. "Get your hands off him. Now," he demands. I take my hands off Silas, but don't move or stand up. Silas sits up, wincing in pain. Before I know it, I'm dragged up by my arm, and then thrown over Reid's shoulder.

"Reid-"

"Not a fucking word, Summer," he growls, and I still. What the fuck did I do? He takes me to his car, and sits me down in the passenger seat none too gently.

"Don't fucking manhandle me," I snap, clicking in my seat belt.

Reid ignores me, starting the car and driving off. After ten minutes of silence, I can't take it anymore.

"What was that?" I say shortly.

"Are you fucking him?" he asks.

My jaw drops open. "What the fuck?"

"Yes or fucking no, Summer," he says, his knuckles white on the steering wheel.

"Fuck you, Reid," I say, looking out the window. I can't believe this shit. I've never even looked at another man the way I look at Reid, never felt for another man what I feel for him, and he doesn't trust me?

"I've been stabbed in the back once or twice, but this takes the fucking cake," he grits out.

"Maybe instead of accusing me, you can tell me what you are talking out?" I say, my voice raising.

"The guy who killed my baby brother, and you're touching him like he's fucking precious? Feeling his face and shit?" he yells, losing control. My mind takes a few seconds to catch up.

Silas is a fighter?

Silas is the one Reece fought?

Lawyer, always in the library studying Silas?

"Reid. Silas is at the library when I study, I had no idea he was the guy! He's studying law, I just thought he was a student!" I try to explain, but it seems Reid's not having it.

"Worst fucking day of my life when I realise Mia was right about you," he says.

I go silent, his words having the effect he wanted them to.

They cut.

Reid is a bastard. I haven't done shit, and I'm not going to take this from him.

"Stop the car," I say, keeping my voice calm and collected.

"You may be a fucking bitch but I'm not a bastard. I'll take you home," he says, his words final.

I dig my nails into my thighs to stop myself from crying.

This is it.

This is the end.

The air in the car feels suffocating, and I open the window a little so I can breathe. Reid's anger is hitting me in waves, as he sits there brooding. I wrap my arms around myself, positioning my body to be as far away from his as possible.

I'm out of the car before he can even come to a full stop.

I don't look back.

I don't hear his car leave until I'm inside the house.

I collapse on my bed, curling into a ball.

Who would have thought my night would end like this?

CHAPTER
TWENTY
ONE

Someone knocks again on my door and I bury myself further under the covers.

"Summer, it's two in the afternoon," I hear my brother say, and I can tell he's worried.

"Come in," I call out, my voice thick with sleep. I spent the night crying, and I must look like shit.

"Hey," he says a little warily. He takes a seat on the end of my bed.

"Hey."

"You okay?" he asks, and I laugh humourlessly.

"No, but I will be."

"You wanna tell me what happened?" he asks gently, relaxing onto the bed. I tell him the story, leaving out Reid's treatment in the car.

"So it was just a misunderstanding, sis. Reid loves you, he'll come around."

He might, but do I want him to?

I force a smile. "We'll see, baby bro. It's not the end of the world, right?" Yeah, I just work for him,

231

and happen to be best friends with his brother. If that's even still the case. The thought makes my heart hurt. If Ryan's mad at me, I don't know what I'll do.

"I'm going to make you some coffee, why don't you get your ass into the shower," he says as he turns to leave.

I get out of a bed with a groan, and then look back down at it longingly. My zebra bed sheets look so welcoming. I sigh heavily, and head for the bathroom. Not even bothering to look into the mirror, I strip down mechanically and hop into an almost scalding fall of water. In my mind, I go through the list of things I need to get done.

First things first. Knox Tavern. I need to find a new job, and stat. I turn the shower off and wrap a towel around me. Still dripping wet, I wipe my hand on the towel before picking up my phone and putting it on speaker.

"Hey, baby girl, I'm just on my way over to see you," comes a gravelly voice.

"Hey, dad. I was wondering, is that job offer still open?"

He's silent for a beat. "Of course it is. But are you sure-"

"Thanks, dad, I'll see you in a bit."

"Alright," he says, sighing.

We both hang up.

I dry myself and dress in a black maxi dress.

"Smells good," I say as I walk into the kitchen. "Never even knew you could cook, Xander."

He laughs. "When the time calls for it."

"Seriously? This whole time!"

He laughs some more. "I wanted my big sister to fuss over me, is that so bad?"

"You owe me," I grumble. Truth be told, I like fussing over him too.

"Your cooking is way better though," he says, grinning.

My lip twitches, and I take a bite of toast. Running through my phone, I scan all the messages in my inbox. Nothing from Reid, not like I expected anything. What hurts the most is nothing from Ryan, either. Dad comes over and we order in pizza for lunch. They're both tip toeing around me, not wanting to bring up Reid's name, and I appreciate it.

After dad leaves I head to the library, not surprised when I see Silas sitting there in his usual seat. He looks worse for wear, and doesn't have any books or folders with him. I sit down opposite him, and stare up at him in silence.

"I knew you were his girlfriend," he starts, and I stay silent. "Reece and I were friends once."

"What happened?" I ask.

He sighs and leans back in his chair. "Jade happened. She was with me first, you know."

I sit up straight. "You fought over Jade?"

"She was my girlfriend, until she wasn't. She left me for Reece."

"You were both into the fighting scene?"

"Yeah, that's how we met." He looks at me for a moment, clearly struggling with what to say.

"I only hit him twice, Summer, fuck. It happened too fast, he went down..." He puts his face into his hands, shaking. After a beat, he looks up. "Look, the reason I was pissed at Reece wasn't just because he stole Jade. If Jade was happy, I was happy. Reece was..." he trails off.

"Tell me," I demand softly.

"Reece was sleeping with Mia, Summer. And I know for a fact her baby is his, not Reid's."

"What?" I ask, gaping. Silas nods sadly, his brown eyes full of regret.

"Mia's a fucking bitch," I snap. Then I realise something. "Jade found out, didn't she? She started acting weird all of a sudden, wanting to move on."

"I guess she did," Silas says, shrugging.

"Reid loves that kid, what the hell am I supposed to do with this?" I ask, my shoulders sagging.

"Ask Jade how she found out?"

"How did you find out?" I ask.

"I overheard Reece and Mia talking before the fight," he says, looking down at the table.

"This is a clusterfuck," I say, puffing out a breath. "You look like shit, Silas. Go home and rest. And... stop punishing yourself," I say softly.

He makes a scoffing sound. "If only, Summer, if only." He gets up and walks out, without looking back.

Right here and now I decide, there's no way in hell I can ever tell Reid about this.

He's not mine to worry about anymore anyway, right?

234

I force myself to study for a few hours and then head home. When I see Ryan's motorcycle parked at my house, I'm extremely surprised. I walk into the house a little warily, not knowing what to expect.

"There you are," he says, standing in the kitchen drinking a juice box.

"Hey."

"How you holding up, babe?" he says, his eyes softening.

"I'm okay."

"You don't look okay," he says knowingly.

"That's not very nice of you to point that out," I snap.

"He's going to realise he fucked up," he says.

"And he's going to be too late," I reply softly, walking to the couch and sitting down. Animal Planet is on, Ryan's favourite channel.

"He was hurt, babe, he'll get over it."

"You're not mad at me?" I ask, turning my head to follow his movements as he walks towards me and takes a seat next to me.

"No. Xander told me what happened, not your fault, babe," he says, pulling gently on a lock of my hair.

"I'm not working for you anymore," I announce.

"Babe-"

"I'll stay for two weeks so you can find someone else."

"Stubborn."

"I'm serious."

"We'll see babe, two weeks is a long time," he says with a sly smile.

"Where is he?" I ask.

"At home in his room, sulking." I lean forward and wrap my arms around Ryan's stomach.

"I'm glad you're not mad at me. I thought you were going to cut me out of your life," I admit.

"Cos my brother overreacted? Don't think so."

"Love you, Ry."

"Love you too, Summer, babe," he says, holding me in his arms.

CHAPTER TWENTY TWO

Four days later, I'm getting dressed for work, dreading having to see everyone, when there's a knock on my door.

"Come in, Xander!" I call out, looking under my bed for my shoe. I find it and cheer, and then glance up at the door.

Reid.

I get up off the floor and scowl. "What are you doing here?" I ask. He looks good. Definitely isn't pining away for me, that's for damn sure.

"We need to talk," he says, rubbing his right hand through his hair. He's cut the sides off even shorter, and the top is thick and full, pushed back on his head.

Fucking hot.

"I'm pretty sure you said all that needed to be said," I say, sitting down on the edge of my mattress.

A flash of remorse passes over his expression. "I fucked up. I saw him, you were touching him, and I lost it." I don't say anything so he continues. "We got into a fight before you and Ryan arrived. I hit him, he

237

didn't even fight back, he just stood there and took it which pissed me off even more." He closes his eyes.

"You realize choosing to fight comes with certain consequences. Silas didn't get into that ring with a plan to kill anyone."

Reid's jaw tightens at my defence of Silas. "I know," he admits quietly after a few tense moments of silence.

"Do you?"

"I'm trying."

Well, that's something, at least.

"Okay, thank you for coming by to explain, Reid," I say, picking up my handbag.

"That's it?" he asks, frowning.

"What, you expected me to run back into your arms after you spoke to me like that? Treated me like that? I'm sorry for what happened, Reid, and I don't know what girls you're used to. But as far as I'm concerned, this right here is done. Now excuse me, cos I gotta get to work," I say, waiting for him to move away from the door.

"I fucked up, baby, it's going to happen. I'm sorry, I never should have spoken to you like that. I love you so fucking much-"

"I gotta go to work, Reid."

"I'll follow you there," he says, trailing me as I walk out.

Xander looks at me and Reid curiously, arching a brow. "Bye, Xander."

"Bye, sis."

I drive to work and Reid follows me on his bike. I turn up the volume on T-Pain's 'Booty Wurk' trying to block out the image of him in my rear view mirror, looking sexy as hell on his bike. I park and exit my car swiftly, walking into the bar without even looking around.

The first people I see are Jade and Tag, who both throw me sympathetic glances. Ryan told me to take a few days off, so this is my first day back at work. The bar is completely dead and spotless. These two must have been bored.

"Hey," I say as I walk in and shove my handbag under the cash register.

"Hey, how you holding up?" Jade asks, looking concerned.

"I'm doing fine, but if someone asks me again, I won't be responsible for my actions," I say, giving them both a threatening glance.

Tag chuckles. "That's the spirit."

Reid takes that moment to walk into the bar, his eyes only for me. I ignore him completely, and start to pour myself a vodka sunrise.

I dare him to say anything about it.

"Happy hour, is it?" he asks, looking amused.

"Figure I'm going to need it. Jade, Tag?" I raise the bottle in question. They both decline, looking back between Reid and me. All they need is popcorn.

"When are you going to forgive me, baby?" Reid asks bluntly, getting straight to the point.

"I'm not."

"Beauty…"

"Mia was right about me, you said. So what exactly did she say about me?" I ask, deciding that if he wanted to have it out right here right now, so be it.

Reid looks uncomfortable and I find myself enjoying watching him squirm a little. "I said I was sorry."

"That isn't what I asked."

"Baby, fuck Mia, who cares what she-"

"Clearly you do since you brought it up that night," I snap, my eyes narrowing.

"She said you were young, immature, untrustworthy... shit like that," he reluctantly admits. And all this coming from a lying, cheating whore. How rich.

"And you agree with those things."

"Summer-"

"You keep saying you fucked up, Reid, but you more than fucked up, you broke my fucking heart. Now, all I need to do is get through these last few shifts, and then I'll never have to see you again."

With that parting comment, I turn and head out the back.

When I return, Reid is gone. Tag stands there watching me and I know he's dying to say something.

"What?"

"I've known Reid for a long time, and I've never seen him put himself out there for a woman like that. You shut him down cold, that was harsh, girl," he says, looking a little disappointed in me.

"You don't know how he treated me that night," I say slowly, my eyes starting to water.

240

"No, I don't, but when you fight you don't need to fight dirty, you're better than that." He walks over and wraps him arms around me. "It's empty here. Why don't you go sit out front for a little while?"

"Okay," I say, taking my drink with me. I take a seat in one of the outside tables, sipping on my drink. I see Reid walk towards me from the car park. Guess he didn't leave after all. He takes the seat right next to me, our shoulders almost touching. I smell a hint of his cologne, and it makes me feel homesick. So close, and yet so far.

Right next to me, but worlds apart.

"You're it for me," he finally says. "I'm not going to give up on you, ever."

I don't reply.

"I'm going to go see River. I'll come and see you tonight," he says, his blue eyes studying me.

River.

My heart shatters.

Jade walks out, looking scared and confused. She gives me a smile that doesn't reach her eyes before walking up to Reid.

"Can you drop me home?" she asks.

He pauses for a moment. "Sure, come on, I'm leaving now." He lowers his head and kisses me on the forehead before he leaves.

I skull the rest of my drink, and then get back to work.

*****

My phone rings in the middle of the night, over and over again. I reach out to pick it up from the side table, but knock it to the ground instead.

"Mother effer."

With an exaggerated groan I get out of bed, and get down on my knees reaching under the bed blindly. I finally find it, only for it to stop ringing. I slide back under my sheets, trying to get warm and comfortable again, when it rings again.

"Yeah?" I answer.

"River isn't mine," Reid says, his voice cracking.

I'm suddenly wide awake.

"What?"

"Jade, she knew, fuck, Summer. I love him, I fucking love him," he says.

I sniffle a little. "He's still your brother's blood, it's okay to love him."

Silence on the other end. "How did you know it was Reece's baby?"

Fuck.

Fuck.

Fuck.

"Reid-"

"Great, my own fucking woman knew, and I didn't, and she didn't even fucking tell me," he growls, his tone a mixture of hurt, pain and anger.

"I found out the day after the fight," I say softly.

"Can't trust anyone these days, can you? My brother was fucking my girlfriend behind my back, and my girl knew and she didn't even tell me," he says bitterly. Salty tears drop down my cheeks.

242

"I love you, Reid, I'm sorry. I know you love River; I didn't want to be the one to break your heart," I say.

"Yeah, well, you just did break my heart, Summer."

"Reid..." I plead.

"I'm done," he says, and he hangs up on me.

He's never hung up on me before.

I quickly call Ryan.

"You knew?" is his answer.

Wow, Reid was quick to tell him that.

"Yeah, I found out the day after the fight," I say.

"This has fucked him up, Summer," he says, sounding worried and a little frantic.

"I'm coming over," I say as I hear a crash in the background.

"Come soon," Ryan pleads softly.

"I'm coming," I say before I hang up. I shove on some track pants under Reid's T-shirt I was sleeping in, and slip my feet into my flats. Grabbing my keys and bag, I drive as quickly as I can while staying under the speed limit. When I get to their apartment and I don't see Reid's bike, I curse. He's driven off somewhere, angry and hurt.

I walk up to their apartment and see their door left wide open. I run through, to find Ryan sitting there at their dining table, his head in his hands.

"Ry?"

He turns to me, and I see the pain in his eyes. I rush over and wrap my arms around him. "Where did he go?"

"I don't know, he just drove off."

"He'll be alright," I try to convince the both of us.

"You didn't see his face, babe." And I don't think I'd want to.

Ryan and I fall asleep on the couch, waiting for him to return.

But he doesn't.

CHAPTER TWENTY THREE

I'm on my way to work when I get an unusual call from Ryan.

"Have you left yet?"

"I'm on my way, why?"

"Well, it's kinda dead here right now, so you don't need to come in," he says. From his tone alone, I can tell that he's lying.

"Okay, I'll see you tomorrow."

The relief is his voice is palpable. "Bye, babe."

I keep driving, wanting to know what the hell is going on. After Reid left that night he hasn't been back to town. It's been a month. He called Ryan twice, and that's about it.

He didn't ring me at all.

My confrontation with Mia wasn't a pleasant one. She came into the bar, looking for Reid. I punched her in the face. Is there underground fighting for women? I may have a career there.

When I see the bar car park full of cars, I scowl. Definitely lying to me. That's when I see it.

Reid's bike.

I park my car and run into the bar. As soon as I walk through the doors, I know why Ryan didn't want me here, and I love him for it.

I wish I'd listened.

Reid is sitting there, with a girl on his lap, straddling him. His hands are on her ass, and his lips are attached to hers. They're basically attacking each other, putting on a big show. His hair is longer, shaggier, and he obviously hasn't shaved since he left.

I look away as I feel tears start to pool in my eyes.

Ryan and Tag both spot me. Ryan's face looks pale, almost as if he can feel my pain. Tag looks straight out pissed off, throwing looks of anger in Reid's direction. What feels like an hour, but has only been a few seconds, pass, and I turn around and leave, needing to get the fuck out of there.

Is this what he's been doing for the last month?

While I've been worrying about him every day?

Instead of going home I go for a drive to clear my head. After driving for an hour, I realise where I'm unconsciously heading.

To my home town.

I message my dad, Xander and Ryan, so they won't worry about where the hell I am. I know I'm going to lose reception soon because a lot of the drive is going through nothing but farm land and bush. I message my friend Sandra, too, to let her know I'll be dropping in. She's going to love it. I put my favourite car CD in, and continue to enjoy the drive.

Reid

"What do you mean she's gone?" I ask, rubbing my eyes. I sit up on the bed, ignoring the pain in my head. *Definitely drank too much last night.*

After spending the last month driving from town to town on my bike, living like a drifter, trying to get my mind straight, I decided to come home. I can't hide and run forever. It's time to face the facts.

River isn't mine, but he is my brother's.

There's a piece of Reece left on this earth, and no matter how he came about, I still love and adore River. He shouldn't have to pay for the sins of his parents.

"After she saw you at the bar last night, she left town," Ryan growls. He starts to pace, running his fingers through his hair, a sure sign of his agitation.

"Why did she leave?" I ask, my mind still foggy from sleep.

Ryan gives me a look I've never seen before from him, and for the first time in my life I wonder if my brother hates me. He stares pointedly at the bed, and I turn my head to see what the fuck he's on about.

A woman.

In bed.

With me.

Fuck.

It all comes back to me.

I'd come back into town, and gone straight to the bar. Everyone had been there, the usual crowd. Mia had also been there. She'd told me, in detail, just how she and Reece hooked up.

247

How it happened.

Why it happened.

It seemed it hadn't even been a one-time thing. My brother and girlfriend were having a full on affair.

And I had no fucking clue.

Then I started drinking. I glance down at the woman in my bed, wondering how the hell I'd fucked up so bad. I put my hands in my face and groan.

Summer. My beautiful Summer.

Fuck, how I've missed her. She didn't deserve this shit. For the first time in a month, I begin to see things clearly. I might not be able to change the past, but I can't keep living there. I need to live for now, for my present and my future.

Summer. I need to live for my Summer.

I stand up with renewed determination.

I gotta fix this and get my girl back.

CHAPTER TWENTY FOUR

"I wasn't the one who got us in trouble, you were!" Sandra yells, followed by giggling.

I laugh, and lean back on the log I'm sitting on. We're sitting outside around a campfire, having a few drinks and reminiscing about old times.

"Is that how you remember it? Cos it's not how I remember it," I say, laughing some more.

Sandra tilts her head back, taking a huge gulp from her bottle which is still wrapped in a brown paper bag. We're so classy. Sandra's short dark hair is tied on the top of her head, her dark eyes framed in her wide glasses.

"It's so boring without you here," she says, sighing.

"I wish we could see each other more often."

"I know, I'm always bloody working," she complains, taking another swig of wine. Sandra works as a personal assistant and is pretty much always on call.

"Your boss needs to loosen his strings," I say, my mouth falling open when I see the look on her face. "What was that face for? What's going on with your boss?"

She looks embarrassed. "We slept together!" she blurts out.

I still. "Sandra what are you thinking?" I scold.

"Like you can talk!"

I think it over. "Touché, Sandra, touché."

We both start laughing again.

"Well, here's a face I didn't think I'd see again," comes a sexy drawl from behind me.

I turn my head. "Quinn! How have you been?"

He looks the same as he did the last time I saw him, except for the fact that his lean, almost lanky build has filled out a little. Tallish with dark shaggy hair, piercing blue eyes and a ring through his eyebrow. Quinn is still a looker, and the boy I gave my virginity to when I was eighteen.

"Good, when did you get back into town?" he asks, kissing me on the cheek and sitting down next to me. I broke up with him a month before I left, after we'd dated for a year. We departed on good terms because I think we both knew we loved each other, but weren't in love with each other. As cliché as that sounds, it was the truth with us.

"I kind of just spontaneously drove up here today."

"Homesick?" he ask kindly, opening a can of beer from the esky.

"Something like that. Thought I'd go to mum's gravestone with some flowers. And see how Sandra's doing," I add. "What are you doing here?"

"Sandra messaged me," he says, looking a little sheepish.

"We're friends, Quinn," I tell him, wanting him to know that it's okay for him to want to see me.

"I know," he says, but I can tell he didn't. He probably thought I'd be awkward about it. My phone rings with a Kings of Leon song, which is Reid's ringtone. I press reject, and put my phone on silent. I just want to forget about him for one night, and he decides to call. This last month I would have given anything for him to call me, or reply to one of my messages, and now I just wish he'd leave me the hell alone.

"Boyfriend?" Quinn asks, a sad smile playing on his lips.

"Not exactly."

"Complicated?"

"Isn't it always?" I say, a little bitterly. I look around. "Where the hell did Sandra go?"

Quinn laughs, a full on belly laugh. "She left as soon as I walked up."

"She's still sneaky, I see. So what have you been up to, Quinn?" I ask, sipping my drink.

"Still at uni studying science, and working part-time," he says, shrugging like it's no big deal.

"I'm proud of you."

He blushes a little. He's so modest. "What are you doing these days? How's living with your brother?" he asks, sounding genuinely interested.

"It's awesome, actually. Xander and I get on really well. And I'm studying to be a nurse, and work in a bar for now."

"That's good. I'm happy for you. When are you heading back?" he asks, bumping me gently with his shoulder.

"Tomorrow."

"That sucks. You girls sleeping out here tonight?" he asks.

"Yeah, just like old times." We used to always camp on Sandra's parents' land, sleeping under the stars. Speaking of the devil, Sandra walks out holding a large container, which I hope has food inside of it.

"I come bearing food!" she calls out.

"Thank God," I reply.

"Sandwiches. I made your favourite, Summer," she says.

"Cheese and tomato," Quinn and I say at the same time. We share a look.

I help Sandra set out the sleeping bags, and we all lay there under the stars, chatting and eating.

A glance at my phone shows eighteen missed called from Reid. I start to worry, thinking something might be wrong, but there are no calls from anyone else, just a message from Ryan saying to be safe. Dad and Xander rang me before, and I told them I was visiting a friend and will be back home tomorrow. They both sounded worried, so I assume they heard the gossip already.

My last thought is of Reid before I fall asleep.

*****

Yellow sunflowers.

My mother's favourite flower. I place down a solitary sunflower on my mother's gravestone. I miss my mum every day, but it hurts that she kept me away from dad and Xander all this time. I think it was selfish of her, and even a little vindictive. She gave me an amazing childhood, though, so I guess I can't really complain. Some people aren't that lucky, to have a mother and father who both love and want them.

My mum died from a heart attack. I still remember the pain of losing her, like it was yesterday. There's no point in looking back, thinking about the 'what ifs'. I decide to think of the fond memories I have with mum, and there really are a lot of them.

"Love you, mum," I say softly, before turning and walking to my car. I slump down into the driver's seat, knowing that it's time to head home.

CHAPTER TWENTY FIVE

Exhausted, I walk slowly to the front door. I have a moment of déjà-vu when Reid opens the door before I can even pull my key out.

"What the fuck are you doing here?" I say, too tired to be dealing with him right now. He says nothing, but moves aside so I can enter. He's shaved the almost beard thing he had going on, but he still looks tired like he hasn't slept.

I walk past him without a word, straight into my room. I slam the door behind me, the force rattling it on its hinges. I quickly lock it, before he can try and enter, and then pull off my denim jacket and fling it onto the ground, and hop straight into my bed. A soft knock alerts me of his presence at my door.

"Summer, can we talk, please?" he begs. His voice contains something I haven't heard in it before, and I frown wondering what it might be. Remorse? Guilt? No, it's *fear*.

"I'm tired, Reid, I just want to sleep. I'm sure your new girlfriend would love to see you, though," I call out, making a grunting noise at my own comment. I

254

hear a tap against the door, and then a sliding noise. I wait ten minutes, and I know he's still there, so I can't even sleep.

"Reid, what are you doing?" I ask.

"I'm going to sit here and wait for you to talk to me," he says. Stubborn man.

"Go home, Reid."

"No."

"I don't want you," I say, frustrated.

"Yeah, well, I want you enough for the both of us," he replies calmly.

"I hate you," I tell him.

"No, you don't, you only wish you did because I'm an asshole." He's an asshole, alright.

"If you love me, you'll just leave me alone."

Silence. Then, "That's bullshit. I do love you, more than anything, and that's why I'm not going to give up."

"If this is how you love someone, by leaving them and cheating on them, then I want no part of your love," I yell, my voice cracking.

I hear him curse. "Please open the door," he rasps. I groan and get up, unlocking the door. Seeing him sitting down on the floor doesn't make me feel good at all.

"Get up, Reid." I say before turning and heading back to bed. He stands up and comes into my room, closing the door behind him. I watch as he sits down on the bed, and his hand reaches up to touch my face.

"I was worried about you," he says quietly.

"Why? It's not like I left for a month with no word," I snap at him.

He breaks eye contact, looking down at his feet. "I was hurting."

"Yeah, well, so was I."

"I reacted badly, beauty, I'm fucking sorry, okay," he says, turning his head back to look at me. He looks sorry, his eyes are sincere, but does it really matter?

"You came to a bar, where you know I work, and had a woman on your lap, making out with her with roaming hands. If I did that to a guy in front of you, how would you feel?" I ask.

His jaw clenches and his eyes harden. "I would seriously hurt whoever the bastard was."

"Yeah, well, I don't do shit like that to you, Reid."

"I was drunk, I'd just seen Mia and she told me things…" he trails off. I can only imagine what Mia had told him. "My head was messed up."

"And I get that. But things don't always go how we want them, are you going to react like this every time a problem arouses?"

"Baby, finding out my baby brother was sleeping with my ex-girlfriend and River is his, not mine, isn't just a problem. It's more than that," he growls, letting his emotions take over.

"You're right," I admit. "I guess I'm just scared now."

"I'll do everything I can to prove to you I'm right for you. No one will ever love you like I do, baby, because it's just not possible. I wanted to do some huge romantic gesture for you, to say sorry, but I'm really not a candles and rose petals kind of guy," he cringes as he says the last few words. "But you know that about me, and you love me anyway. So I was hoping," he swallows heavily. "I was hoping, you would give me another chance. I won't lose you, Summer. I can't."

He takes my hand into his, and threads our fingers together.

His large hand enveloping my small.

"I kissed that girl in the bar. I didn't even know who she was. And then when I woke up in the morning, she was next to me in the bed," he says. I gasp and pull my hand out of his.

"You f-"

"Let me finish, baby. We were both fully dressed and I spoke to her, nothing happened. I promise. She said we came home and passed out because I was drunk. The only thing we did was what you saw in the bar, and I know that that's bad enough, because it would absolutely kill me so see you be like that with someone else, but it didn't go any further than that," he says.

I curse. "I don't know if I can trust you anymore."

"Give me a chance to prove myself. I know I'll have to work for it, and I'm willing to do anything I can," he pleads softly.

"What about River?" I ask, biting my bottom lip.

He looks at me strangely. "I love River. He's my nephew, and I'm still going to be in his life. I'm going to take care of him."

"Good," I whisper.

"I don't expect you to forgive me right now, but at least let me know you'll give me a chance to make it up to you," he says, placing his hand gently on the side of my face. I don't answer, but move aside for him to hop into the bed. I can't make any promises, so I won't. His eyebrows go up and I know he was sure I was going to kick his ass out. He smiles sweetly, and hops into the bed. With an arm around my waist he pulls me in close to his body. I know we could both use the rest, because we both look like crap right now.

"I'm so in love with you, Summer. I don't think that will ever change," he says into my hair.

My eyes close as I fall into deep sleep.

*****

I wake up groggily, feeling like I didn't sleep at all. Sitting up in the bed, I rub my eyes, and then stretch lazily.

"Morning," I say, when I see Reid sitting on the edge of the bed, staring at the wall. He's taken his shirt off, and is wearing nothing but his jeans. The muscles on his back flex as he stands up, but he still doesn't face me.

"What's wrong?" I ask. I grab my phone and check the time. Holy shit, I've been asleep for five hours. He finally turns to face me. He looks stricken, and a little pissed off.

"What is it, Reid?" I demand.

"Your phone rang and I answered it," he grinds out.

"Okay? And?" I ask, shaking my head in confusion.

"It was Quinn. Asking if you got home okay," he says. I pretend I don't see his clenched fists or set jaw.

"Really, well, that was nice of him," I say, getting out of bed.

"That's all you're going to say?"

"Yeah, pretty much."

"You went and spent the night with your ex?" he asks, and the flash of pain on his face is my undoing.

"Could you blame me if I did?" I ask quietly.

"No, I guess not. But it still hurts," he admits, exhaling deeply.

"Yes, I saw him. Nothing happened. We just hung out," I say.

"Thank fuck," he mutters, taking me into his arms, almost squashing me. "The thought of someone else touching you. Fucking hell, beauty, you drive me crazy."

"The feeling is entirely mutual, trust me," I say dryly.

"Good to know," he says, a faint smile making an appearance.

"You going home now?" I ask.

"Yeah, you wanna come with me? Ryan's been calling non-stop," he says, sounding a little unsure.

"Using your brother as a weapon, huh?" I tease.

"I'll use anything and everything I can to get what I want, you know that," he says, smirking.

"And I'm what you want?"

"Always."

"Okay, let me have a shower first," I say.

"Okay?" he repeats.

"Yeah, okay," I say, offering him a small grin.

I start to walk down the hall, and turn back to find him leaning against the wall, smiling.

CHAPTER TWENTY SIX

A woman walks out of Ryan's room, a smile on her pouty lips. Ryan walks out behind her, his face lighting up when he sees me.

"You're back."

"I am."

"Good," he says, leaning in to kiss me.

"Who knows where those lips have been, Ryan Knox," I say, making a face.

Ryan and Reid laugh, while the woman makes a stealthy exit. "Glad you two sorted your shit out, babe."

"Well, we're working on it," I say, smiling up at the both of them.

"Good, give him hell," he says, smirking. Reid slaps him on the back of the head. "I gotta get to the bar. You coming in tonight, Summer?"

"Yeah, I'll come in for a few drinks," I say.

"Perfect." He grabs a green apple from the fruit bowl and taking a huge bite out of it, then points it at me. "I'll see you later, then."

CHANTAL FERNANDO

Ryan leaves, and I look at Reid who is already watching me. "What are you staring at?" I ask playfully.

"You. We've never had make up sex before," he says, sinking his teeth into his bottom lip. His gaze roams my body, my tight black top and short denim skirt.

"Is that right?" I ask.

"Yeah, and baby, I really want under that skirt," he says in a low, husky tone. He stares at my thighs and licks his lips. I start walking backwards, backing away to the bedroom. Stalking me like prey, Reid grins. "You wanna play, do you, beauty?"

Without answering, I run to his room, laughing when he catches me around my waist and lifts me in the air.

"Missed you so much," he says in between kisses. "So fucking much."

"Missed you, too."

"Nothing compares to this, to you," he growls, kissing me deeply.

"Show me how much you missed me," I demand, lifting my hips up so he can pull off my skirt.

"Oh, I'll show you," he growls, tearing my panties off. Well, that's a first. Pulling his shirt off, he tosses it on the floor. I stare at him hungrily, my eyes devouring his chiselled body.

"You keep staring at me like that, you better be in the mood for rough," he says huskily, nibbling on his lip. I tilt my head, flashing him a come hither smile, and watch as he leans on the bed, cupping my face with his hands.

"You want this?" he asks, kissing my lips. While his lips consume mine, his fingers roam. My hips buck when he starts caressing me in the perfect spot.

"You know I do," I respond breathily. He pulls down his pants and slides into me slowly, savouring the pleasure. When he's fully inside me, he thrusts a few times, then rolls onto his back so I'm straddling him.

"Fuck me," he growls, and I comply eagerly. Lifting my hips, I slide up and down. I lift my head back and lean my arms on his thighs, using them as an anchor. He curses as I start to move faster, grinding down on him in a sensual rhythm. His fingers dig into my hips, urging me faster. We finish together, our eyes locked together as each wave of pleasure hits.

It turns out although I hate fighting with Reid, I really love the make-up sex.

*****

"Thanks for telling him the truth, Jade, cos there's no way in hell I could have," I tell her, running my finger through the frost on the outside of the glass.

She looks down into her own drink. "It was hard. It was fucked up. But I had to do it, it was eating me alive," she admits.

I nod, because I felt the same way. "So, you and Silas, huh?"

She grunts. "Something like that." Sounds like there's more to that story.

I lift my drink up at Tag, signalling that I need a refill. He grins and starts to pour me another.

"So, you and Reid, even after his performance the other night," she says, lifting a blonde, finely arched brow.

"Something like that," I repeat her words. "We still have a lot to work out." And we do. We need to rebuild the trust in our relationship. But he's up to the task, and so am I.

"Reid still going to fight Silas?" she asks. Good question.

"Not if I have anything to do with it," I answer. She's about to reply when we see a woman walk into the bar.

She is possibly the hottest woman I have ever seen in my life. Curly chocolate brown hair, green eyes and olive skin, she looks like she might have a mixed heritage. Her body is shapely and feminine, with a tiny waist and gently flared hips. She's a knock out.

I watch as she storms up to Ryan, anger evident in her tight expression and quick paced steps. Ryan scowls when he sees her, and walks around the bar, pulling her into a corner. They have a hushed argument, where I assume Ryan says something stupid, because she slaps him across the face before she walks out. Ryan stands there, looking stunned and angry, rubbing his cheek.

"Who was that?" I ask, wide eyed.

Jade looks as stunned as I do. "I don't know, but I hope she comes back."

Reid and Tag are laughing their asses off at Ryan. Ryan walks into the office and slams the door. Interesting. I've never seen a girl get him riled up before, or make him show any emotion. He's nothing but charming in their presence, at all times.

Reid walks over and sits down next to me.

"Ryan needs to wife that woman."

He gives me a funny look, taken aback. "Why do you say that?" His tone is curious.

"Did you see her? She's fucking hot!"

Reid laughs. "Not as hot as you, baby, trust me."

It's true. Love is blind.

"You wanna get out of here?" he asks, holding his hand out to me.

"Yeah, I do."

"Good, I have plans for you tonight," he says, his eyes twinkling.

"Just for tonight?"

"For every night, baby."

I like the sound of that.

EPILOGUE

Three years later

"River, the movie's started!" I call out. River runs into the lounge room, holding his new toy Reid bought him.

"What movie are we watching Aunty Summer?" he asks in his cute little voice.

"Teenage Mutant Ninja Turtles," I say, handing him some popcorn.

"Again?" he asks, frowning.

I laugh. "We can change it if you like."

Reid walks in and smiles at the two of us sitting there.

"Uncle Reid!" River calls out. He loves Reid.

The last few years have been amazing. Reid and I worked hard on our relationship, and we're stronger than ever. He never did fight Silas, or anyone else ever again. He still trains to keep fit, though, and there's no way I'm going to complain about that.

River spends every second weekend with us, and we love having him here. Last month Reid proposed, and, of course, I accepted. We moved into a bigger house, and Ryan moved right next door. It's the perfect set up, and the best of both worlds.

Reid looks at the TV. "Again?" he asks me, frowning.

I laugh again. "Fine, you guys choose something, then."

"How about we go out?" Reid offers.

"Sounds good," I say, looking down at River. "You wanna go to the arcade?" I ask him, knowing it's his favourite place to go.

His scream of happiness is all the answer we need.

"I'm going to kick your butt in air hockey," I boast to Reid.

"You wish, baby," he says, chuckling.

"Let's go get Ryan to come with us."

"Of course."

We walk out of the house, each of us holding one of River's hands.

Sneak peak at Ryan's book! Coming in 2014

THIS TIME AROUND

by
Chantal Fernando

Ryan

When she walks in, I'm surprised. No, I'm shocked. I never thought I'd see the day that she walked back into this bar, but here she is. Her curly brown hair frames her round face, and her blazing green eyes are narrowed in anger. Even angry, she's the most beautiful woman I've ever been in the presence of. My gaze can't help but wander down her shapely body. She's stacked in all the right places, and I should know, I've tasted every inch of her body many times over. She steps in front of me and purses her lips.

"You had no right, Ryan," she seethes, her voice low and shaking.

"I had every right," I reply calmly, pretending this woman has no effect on me. When in truth, she owns me, body and soul.

Only she doesn't know it.

"I'm not yours anymore," she says, her voice losing its edge. She sounds resigned, tired. I don't like it one bit. I prefer her anger.

"I had you first, you'll always be mine," I say with a shrug.

She shakes her head. "Leave him alone, Ryan, I'm serious. You can't keep doing this to me."

I lean in a little closer so I can smell her familiar scent. "Tell him to leave you alone then, Taiya."

"So, you get to fuck anything with a skirt, but a good man can't even look my way?" she asks, gritting her teeth.

"Yeah, that pretty much sums it up."

I don't expect the slap. But I should have. Taiya always did have a fiery temper on her.

"Fuck you, Ryan, stay out of my life," she spits out before storming off.

I watch her walk away from me.

My wife.

I should be used to it by now, but it still hurts.

It always hurts.

More Than This

Book One in the More Series
by Jay McLean

Prologue

He was right. It made no difference whether it was 6 months or 6 years.

I couldn't undo what had been done. I couldn't change the future. I couldn't even predict it.

It was one night.

One night when everything changed.

It was so much more than just the betrayal.

It was the Tragedy.

The Deaths.

The Murders.

But it was also that feeling.

That feeling of falling.

Chapter One

Mikayla

I finish getting ready with fifteen minutes to spare. I look in the mirror to make sure everything's in place. I'm nothing special to look at. I'm definitely no Megan, my best friend. I have naturally olive skin from being quarter Filipino on my mom's side, and slightly almond shaped eyes from that side, too. Everything else is from Dad's Irish/Scottish side. My dad's six foot, my mom's a tiny five-foot-nothing. Luckily, I'm a good in-between.

I'm not naive in thinking that I'm popular based on looks or extra-curricular activity. I'm book smart, but not so much so that I'm socially awkward. I've made the popular list by association. My best friend is the head cheerleader, and my hot boyfriend is captain of our basketball team.

I take one more look in the mirror. I'm good to go.

I open my bedroom door and virtually run into my parents who are standing just outside. They have that look on their face, like whatever they're about to say is imperative and has to be taken seriously. My dad's arm is wrapped around Mom's shoulders. Emily, my nine-year-old little sister, is nowhere to be seen. They take a step forward, united, causing me to take a step back.

I'm officially worried.

They keep taking steps forward, until I'm forced to sit on the edge of my bed. I look up at my parents.

They finally let go of each other, and sit on either side of me.

Dad blows a big breath out and shakes his head. "Honey, your mother and I have something we need to tell you."

I look at my mom, she looks away. She's nervous.

Shit.

Dad continues, "We figure since you're graduating in two weeks, and you've been eighteen for a few months now ... well, I guess we both decided it was about time we tell you something very important."

I'm mentally scanning my brain for what the fuck this could be.

I'm adopted.

I knew it. I was always different, less Asian looking than I should be, and I don't know where my nose comes from. No one in my family has this nose. Oh, God. Who are my birth parents? And Emily, what about her ... is she adopted too?

"Mikayla?" Dad interrupts my raging thoughts.

Shit.

I close my eyes, hoping that by doing so, it might take away the sting of what he's about to tell me. "Are you listening to me?"

I nod once, eyes still closed.

"Mikayla." There's a long pause. "Boys have a penis…"

My eyes dart open. My dad's stifling a laugh, my mom's face is beet red with held in laughter. I'm glaring at them with narrowed eyes, waiting for my pulse rate to decrease.

I would have bet a million frickin dollars they were about to tell me something life altering.

I want to junk punch my own dad.

I know he's behind this shit. This is totally something he would do. My mom, she doesn't have it in her to think of something like this.

As I'm about to stand, so I can turn and face them both, Emily comes running into the room with her life size Justin Bieber cardboard cut out. She's hiding behind it, cackling to herself. Then she breaks out in song, waving the cut out in front of her.

"And I was like penis, penis, penis, ohhhhh! Like penis, penis, penis, nooooo! Like penis, penis, penis, ohhhh! I thought you'd always be mine, mine!"

I'm trying so hard to hold in my laughter, in case this is one of those situations where it's funny for us, but inappropriate for a nine-year-old girl.

I look to my parents and wait for their reaction.

Mom giggles, and Dad breaks out in a weird dance, which I'm pretty sure is supposed to be something resembling 'The Dougie', and starts to belt out, "You know you love me, I know you caaaare!"

I can't help but laugh. I start down the stairs to wait for Megan and James, shaking my head at their craziness. Of course, they all follow, Justin Bieber cut out and all, and keep singing, at the top of their lungs, mom included.

"And I was like penis, penis, penis, ohhhhh! Like penis, penis, penis, nooooo! Like penis, penis!"

The front door swings open.

"What the fuhhhhhh—" Megan's words die in the air when she sees Emily—and the Biebs—behind me.

James scratches his head. "Are you guys singing about penises? To Justin Bieber?"

They all start laughing and snorting. I love my insane family.

***

After a good ten minutes of photos, and my dad retelling the humiliation of the shit they just pulled on me, we're out of the house, and on our way to Bistro's. It's an Italian restaurant downtown that's famous for loud atmosphere and big tables for large groups. Perfect for pre-prom dinner.

When we get to the restaurant, we notice a few other tables with kids our age, all dressed up. We don't recognize them; they must go to different schools. The place reeks of new garments, cheap cologne, overpowering perfume, hair product and sexual tension. It's everything prom should be.

We find our table and sit with Andrew and Sean, two of James' friends from his Basketball team, and their girlfriends.

Megan decided to go stag. It wasn't like she hadn't been asked, because about a trillion different guys asked her. She said she wanted to keep her options open. She didn't want to go with some guy because he was hot, only to find out he was a dick throughout the night and then have to put out at the end—*her words*.

We make small talk until the waiter comes and takes our order. The place is loud with conversation, like you would expect with a bunch of teenagers in the room. Once we've all placed our order, James stands up, "Where's the toilet in this place? I need to take a leak, that champagne from the limo's gone straight through me."

He's charming, as always.

"I'll show you, since I need to use the ladies to re-adjust my underwear. It's riding up my ass," Megan states loudly.

They walk away towards the back of the restaurant, where the restrooms are.

I'm in the middle of talking to Andrew about the new gym they're building at the school, when I feel something wet trickle down my back. I'm frozen for a second, then turn to find some dude in a tux looking at me wide eyed, half a glass of beer in his hand. The other half, I'm sure, is down my back.

"Shit, babe. I'm sorry," wide-eyed douchebag says.

Babe? Really? This guy has to be a joke.

"Jesus Christ, Logan. Turn down the asshole a little, would ya?" his friend behind him says. He has an accent, like English, or South African, or Australian or something.

Logan, I assume, turns around to face his friend so quickly, his hand holding the remains of his beer slams against accent-boy's broad chest. Beer spills on the crispy white shirt under his open tux jacket. Logan stifles a laugh. Accent boy groans, and pushes Logan to the side, heading to the back of the restaurant, towards the restrooms I presume.

"Naw, don't be like that, Jakey," Logan mocks.

I stand up to go to the restroom to see if this night, or the dress is worth salvaging, but Douchebag Logan blocks my way. He eyes me up and down, and walks a slow circle around me. He comes to a stop in front of me, and a small smirk pulls at his lips.

"Well, hello there, little lady," he drawls.

I physically push him out of the way, and head towards the restroom. I'm wearing a backless dress. It's halter style, all black, it reconnects just above my ass, so close that there's no room for underwear, just in case. Because of this, I'm hoping, fingers crossed, that the beer has just spilt just on my back, and not the dress. I'll be able to clean my bare back at least. More than I can say for the kid with the accent.

As I turn into the hallway where the restrooms are, I stop in my tracks. Megan is halfway out the door of the ladies room. She's adjusting her dress slightly, her hair is in shambles, and her lipstick is smeared all around her lips. She's giggling, and her hands come up slowly, most likely to the face of some random guy she's just hooked up with.

Megan is every guys walking wet dream. She's your typical tall, leggy, blond haired, blue eyed, sex on legs. And she loves sex, and has sex—*so much sex*.

So, it doesn't surprise me at all that we've been here all of fifteen minutes and she's been doing God knows what, with some random dude, in a public bathroom. What does surprise me, though, as I get closer to her, is that it's not some random guy her hands are on. It's James. *My* boyfriend. Her hands are on his face, cleaning the smeared lipstick from around his mouth. My eyes are drawn to his hands, which are at the front of his pants. He tucks 'himself' back in, and does his fly up.

I feel the vomit creeping up my throat, and make a noise trying to keep it down. The noise must be loud enough to distract them. It almost feels like slow motion, they both turn to face me at the same time, their eyes huge, mouths hanging open.

Like they're surprised *I'm* intruding on *their* intimate fucking moment.

ABOUT THE AUTHOR

Amazon bestselling author Chantal Fernando is 26, a mother of three beautiful little boys and lives in Western Australia. Chase is her debut novel, followed by Kade, Ryder & James. She is currently working on 'Spin My Love' a new adult contemporary romance, along with a few other projects.

Chantal loves to hear from readers! You can find her here:

Facebook author page:

https://www.facebook.com/authorchantalfernando

XOXO

Made in the USA
Lexington, KY
28 September 2015